MW01103990

SHADOW MAN

Books by Cynthia D. Grant
Kumquat May, I'll Always Love You
Phoenix Rising: Or How to Survive Your Life
Keep Laughing
Shadow Man

SHADOW MAN

BY CYNTHIA D. GRANT

Atheneum   1992   New York

Maxwell Macmillan Canada
Toronto

Maxwell Macmillan International
New York   Oxford   Singapore   Sydney

Atheneum
Macmillan Publishing Company
866 Third Avenue
New York, NY 10022

Maxwell Macmillan Canada, Inc.
1200 Eglinton Avenue East
Suite 200
Don Mills, Ontario M3C 3N1

Macmillan Publishing Company is part of the Maxwell Communication
Group of Companies.

First edition
Printed in the United States of America
10 9 8 7 6 5 4 3 2 1
The text of this book is set in 11 point Baskerville.

Book design by Tania Garcia

Library of Congress Cataloging-in-Publication Data

Grant, Cynthia D.
    Shadow man / Cynthia D. Grant. — 1st ed.
        p.   cm.
    Summary: Charming but reckless eighteen-year-old Gabe, drunk as
usual, smashes his truck into a tree and dies, sending waves of shock
and grief through his small town.
    ISBN 0-689-31772-7
    [1. Death—Fiction.   2. Family problems—Fiction.   3. Alcoholism—
Fiction.]   I. Title
PZ7.G76672Sh   1992
[Fic]—dc20   91-36054

For my son Morgan, who eggs me on,
sometimes with real eggs

For his wonderful pop, Daniel

For a beautiful woman, Patti Lewis,
and for Ann Boone, a real teacher

What man of you, if his son asks for bread,
will give him a stone?

Matthew 7:9

SHADOW MAN

1

Jennie Harding

Something terrible has happened, but I don't believe it. They say Gabriel is dead.

The phone woke me up a couple of hours ago. My mother picked it up in the hallway.

The sky was getting light. I was drifting back to sleep. Then I heard her cry out, "Oh, my God!"

I got out of bed and opened the door so I could hear my mother talking. "Oh my God, oh my God, oh my God," she kept saying, as if the news were breaking over her in waves.

Then she said, "She's still asleep. I'll tell her later." Before their bedroom door closed she told my father: "That was Betsy Shahl. Gabriel's dead. He smashed his pickup into a tree."

Dreaming, caught between darkness and light, I dressed quickly, pulling on my blue sweater and the skirt Gabe likes so much. In minutes I was out of the house, glad I'd brought a jacket. The morning was cool. The streets were empty. Everyone was inside, getting ready for work or school.

I walked fast, trying not to think. There was no need to panic. Mrs. Shahl is a gossip. She has a knack for making things sound bad. I wouldn't think about anything until I talked to Gabe. I planned to meet him at our special place. That's where he'd come to find me.

But somehow I ended up on the dirt road that leads to his house. I was surprised when I saw it, dead ahead, beyond the little pond in the front yard. Cars and trucks were parked all around. Some don't run, some are for sale, some belong to his brothers, but Gabe's pickup was gone, so I knew he wasn't there.

Jack must've seen me. I heard him barking in the house. I took off before anyone came to see what he was fussing about. I didn't want to talk to Gabe's brothers or his father and get them all worked up for nothing.

Gabe can't be dead. It will turn out to be a rumor. Mrs. Shahl probably fell asleep next to her police scanner and dreamed up the accident. She's always the first one with news of disasters: a burning barn, a child in a well, some fool driving too fast in the fog and plunging off the highway into the ocean. We lose a few tourists that way, their being in a hurry to be someplace else.

I count my steps, keeping my mind busy. How will I explain cutting school today? I heard this terrible rumor, I'll say, and it really upset me. I love school. I'm a good student. When I graduate next year, I plan to go to Chico or Davis or maybe even Berkeley, if they'll take me.

Gabriel and I won't be staying in Willow Creek. It's a nice town, but we've lived here forever. Gabe has anyway. We moved here when I was eight.

I want to do important things. I want to see exciting places. But I want Gabriel to go with me.

He says, "What the hell would I do in a city, a rough old boy like me?" Smiling when he says it so I know he's teasing. He could get a good job, he's so smart and quick; he can learn anything in a minute. And I'll go to college and get my teaching certificate—

O Gabriel, please. O Gabriel, please. I need to have you with me right now.

I've been walking for a long time, through misty woods, tender ferns unfurling under ancient trees; now through a meadow that is purple with lupine and swept with incredibly yellow Scotch broom. May is such a pretty month. Nothing could go wrong today. This summer I'm going to work in the library. We'll save our money. I'll get scholarships. I know Mrs. Sanders will recommend me. She's the very best teacher I've ever had. Someday I hope someone will say the same for me.

The fog is lifting. I can see the ocean. A car is coming down the highway, so I step behind a tree. If people saw me, they'd say, Jennie Harding, what are you doing way out here? Then they'd guess that I was going to meet

Gabe, and our secret place wouldn't be a secret anymore. The car was full of strangers. I should've known by the make. This is Chevy and Ford country, with lots of pickups like Gabe's. That thing may be old, but it's his baby.

School must be starting. The sky is pinky blue. Although I've been walking for miles, I'm not tired. I could meet Gabe in hell if I had to.

I hear a truck coming. I turn around. I'd know the sound of that engine anywhere. It's Gabriel. He stops the truck beside me. Jack is in the back, wagging his tail.

Gabe opens the truck door and pulls me in beside him. I bury my face in his neck, his hair. I knew you wouldn't leave me, I say, crying.

Well, of course I wouldn't leave you. He's puzzled, smiling. Why are you so sad, honey girl?

I wish as hard as I can—I can see him in my mind, I can feel his arms around me! But the highway is deserted.

Just ahead is the place where we park the truck. No one can see it from the road. It's screened by a thicket of blackberry bushes. The truck could be there now, for all I know.

It's not.

Gabriel is always late.

A hundred yards down the highway is the tuck in the cliffs, where the path leads down to the sea. It's steep and slick; it wouldn't be safe for anyone but Gabe and me.

Maybe he wrecked the truck and has come on foot. He'll be so upset, because he loves that truck, and he knows how mad his dad will be. As if Mr. McCloud has a right to talk. He wrecked a lot of cars when he was still drinking.

I leave the highway and am on the path, but I can't see the beach yet or our special place. That's where he'll wait for me. Just beyond that clump of wildflowers, I'll look down and see Gabe. I have to take my time or I'll lose my balance. It's a long drop to the rocks below.

2

Donald Morrison

The ambulance arrived at about six o'clock. My father stuck his head in my door and said, "Get up, Donald. I need you."

I was already awake; they'd had the siren going, for some stupid reason. It's enough to wake the dead, people say, but it's not.

"Who is it?" I asked.

"Gabe McCloud," he said, and left.

I felt like I couldn't get out of the bed; like my legs had been cut off. Gabe McCloud dead. Jennie would die when she found out. She would curl up into a ball and die. If she hadn't already been killed too.

I dressed and went downstairs. My father was talking to the ambulance attendants.

"Gabe McCloud. Big surprise, huh?" the driver said.

My father just grunted and signed some papers. "You know where to put him. Donald, unlock the back doors."

The bodies are always delivered around back, like sides of beef to a restaurant.

I said, "Was Jennie with him?"

My father gave me a look. I turned to the ambulance driver.

"Was anyone else hurt?"

"No, he was all by his lonesome."

"Get the doors, Donald," my father said again.

I'd forgotten my keys. I went back upstairs, feeling as if I were moving underwater. You'd think I'd be used to people dying, but I'm not. No matter how old I get, I'll never be like my father.

By the time I got downstairs my father had opened the doors. The men had left Gabe on the stainless steel table. My father was looking down at him.

"What's the matter with you?" he said to me. "Is this some friend of yours?"

"Not exactly." Jennie's my only real friend. We've always been close, even though I'm a few years older. But I'd always liked Gabe. He was so full of life. Now all the life had leaked out of him.

"Will you pull yourself together? Look at the way you're dressed. You didn't even put on a tie. This is a business, Donald. People expect us to be professionals. How will you ever take over when I'm gone?"

I won't, I could've told him. I will never run this business. When you die, it will be your funeral pyre. I'll burn this place to the ground.

`

"Are you going to give me a hand, or are you going to stand around looking tragic? Bring me the tray."

I couldn't bear to look at Gabe. Once he was so tall and strong and golden.

I brought the tools my father required.

"Gabe McCloud," he said. "Oh, how the mighty have fallen." Then he rolled up his sleeves and went to work.

3

Tom Dawson

When the phone rang, the wife said, "Don't answer it," her voice as sharp in the darkness as if she'd been waiting for the call.

"I have to answer it."

"No, you don't."

"Somebody has to go out on these calls."

She said, "Why does it have to be you?"

We went all through this before we got married. I thought Becky understood. But lately when the phone rings she gets all worked up. Be careful of the fog, she says. Don't drive too fast. As if I hadn't lived here all my life.

"What's up?" I said into the phone.

"You, just barely," said Lois, the dispatcher. "Somebody hit a tree, a mile south of Widow's Peak."

"Dead or alive?"

"Don't know," she said. "A trucker called it in."

I got out of bed and dressed. One of the boys woke up. Becky brought him a glass of water.

By the front door she asked, "How long will you be gone?"

"Depends what we find." I hugged and kissed her. "Go back to bed."

"I can't sleep without you."

"Yes, you can," I said firmly. "Now promise me."

I'm old enough to be her father and at that moment, I felt it. I'll be dead on my feet at the store tomorrow. I've been a volunteer fireman since I was twenty. Too long. It used to be exciting. You rush down to the station and the sirens are blaring. You jump on the truck and it rolls. Your armpits prickle as you roar down the road, wondering if you'll find life or death, a mangled stranger or your own mother. But now I'm getting too old.

Roger and Stan were suiting up at the station. Stan's a new man, young and green, but Roger's been around. I trust him. I put on my gear and we took off.

As soon as we got past Widow's Peak we could see there was no need to hurry. A pickup truck was wrapped around a tree. One headlight was burning through the fog.

We walked toward the truck. The night was real quiet, except for the sound of the sea. Suddenly I got this sickening feeling. "Oh, Lord," Roger said. "It's Gabe Mc-Cloud."

He was dead. The steering wheel was stuck in his chest, but there wasn't a lot of blood.

"I guess he got where he was going," Stan said. "Look at this." The front of the pickup was full of empty beer cans and there were a bunch more in the bed. "Poor little dumb-ass. I've seen him around town. I hear his family's nothing but trouble."

I said nothing. There was nothing to say. Roger said, "Where the hell is the ambulance?"

We've been having a problem with the ambulance lately. It won't start without some fooling around under the hood. Which is fun when you're supposed to be rushing someone to the county hospital. In Gabe's case, there was no rush.

I didn't want him to be dead. He's a good kid, nothing like his old man or his brothers. Why couldn't it have been Fran or one of them? I felt like I was going to throw up.

When the ambulance came, we got Gabe out of the truck. It was a mess; he was really stuck. The whole time, I tried not to think who it was, 'cause when I did, I felt like screaming. Gabe used to be such a happy kid. He could really cheer you up.

We rode back to town. Gabe went over to the mortuary. I arranged for his truck to be towed to the Chevron so I could clean it up before his mother saw it.

Then there was nothing to do but drive home. All these thoughts crowded into my mind. I kept picturing Gabe when he was little, bright as a dime; he was different from his brothers. The other two take after Franny, especially the middle one, Gerald. He's bad news.

They say Franny's changed since he stopped drinking. I don't know. He and I don't talk anymore. After that car deal, I wrote him off. Selling me a piece of junk like that.

I used to think Gabe would amount to something, if he lived long enough to straighten out. He did the damnedest, dumbest things, like quitting school this year. One semester to go and he drops out, as if he couldn't imagine graduating, as if he had to be a failure.

At least he wasn't mean. There's no excuse for meanness. Fran should rot in hell for the way he treated those boys. Beating them bloody, beating up their mother. We all knew it was going on. A couple of times people even called the county and reported it to one of those child abuse places. Nothing came of it. The county seat's too far away. They don't care what's going on in Willow Creek.

Things changed when the boys got big. Gerald fractured Franny's skull with a pool cue one time. David beat him up in a bar. But if an outsider attacked them, they'd stick together like molasses. People used to pray they'd move away. Except for Gabe. Everybody loved Gabe. He used to love to sing, even when he was a baby: He'd sing the little jingles he heard on TV.

Makes me sick to think about it. Makes my stomach hurt and my blood pound and my eyes ache from not crying. I'm lying in bed, Becky's head on my chest, her breath warm and even. She's sleeping. She was waiting up for me when I got home. When I told her what had happened she started crying.

"Was he wearing his seat belt?" she asked.

"No, he wasn't wearing his seat belt! Are you kidding?

12

If he'd had one, he wouldn't have worn it. That's how stupid they all are!"

"I'm sorry, honey. I was just asking." Becky's voice trembled. I felt ashamed. It wasn't her fault that Gabriel was dead.

I hugged her. "I didn't mean to yell," I said. "I'm just tired. Let's go to bed."

That was an hour ago. The curtains hold back the light. But I can't fall asleep; I'm too exhausted.

It's funny, a little while ago, for a second I thought I was holding Kay instead of Becky. Kay died of cancer when our boys were in tenth grade. Now they're grown up with families of their own, and Becky and I have two little boys. . . . Sometimes it's hard to keep things straight. Sometimes I feel like I fell asleep and when I woke up, my whole life had changed. Kay's gone, the twins are grown men, Becky's here, and I'm forty-eight—

Damn it, Gabe, you poor little baby. You never even knew what hit you.

4

Jennie Harding

Gabe's not here yet. He'll show up any second.

I can feel him with me. I can feel how much he loves me. He can't have gone out of this world.

The sun has warmed the rock I'm sitting on. The ocean spreads around me like a blue skirt, the color shifting in the light, reflecting sky. I'd never walked here before. It must've been ten miles. Good thing I wore my comfortable shoes.

Gabe always talks about hiding food on the beach; burying a treasure chest full of goodies so that when we get hungry, there it will be and we won't have to drive back to town. He hasn't gotten around to that yet, but the hole in my stomach isn't hunger, it's worry. If Gabe is really dead—

He's not, he's fine. God wouldn't let somebody like Gabriel die.

Oh, Gabe, I'd be so scared if I thought you'd left me.

The sun feels like gentle fingers on my face. The sea

14

is calm. It's a perfect day for diving. Gabe will probably be here in his wet suit soon, hungry for abalone.

I get upset if he dives when the ocean is rough. He's not afraid of the water. But he knows you have to respect it. The ocean fills me with awe. Think of it, wrapped around the planet, touching everything, like God.

I've seen Gabe and his dog standing on the sea, on a rock that was almost gone; waves crashing over them, Jack barking, scared. He hates being out there, but he won't desert his master. Get out of there! I'm screaming. Gabe's smile is gleaming. He throws his head back to drain his can of beer. Then he jumps into the water—

He always makes it back to shore. By then I'm frantic, angry.

What's the matter with you? I yell at him. Do you want to get killed?

He grins.

It feels so odd to be here on a school day. Gabriel thinks I take school too seriously. It floors me when he says that school's not important. You've got to have a good education. Do you want to work in a mill all your life, I say, making coffins and losing your hearing?

What? Gabe shouts. You'll have to speak up!

He's too smart to play dumb. He's brilliant. And I'm not just saying that because I love him. Mrs. Sanders thinks so too, even though he's always had problems with school. She thinks he might have a learning disability; but Gabe's not interested in being tested. He says he's done all right so far.

His family is a big part of the problem. They think school is a waste of time. His mother didn't care when he dropped out. She didn't want him going away to college; she wanted him to stay in town. My parents are the opposite. Their biggest fear is that I'll marry Gabe and settle down here and get a job selling hot dogs at the drive-in.

We do want to marry, but we have big plans. Big plans! Gabe laughs when he hears me say that.

Judging by the sun, I'd guess it's almost nine. I've been out on the rock for about an hour. The first time Gabriel showed me this place, I was afraid to come out here. I'm not the world's best swimmer. He told me that it's perfectly safe, as long as you keep track of the time. When the tide is low we simply cross from shore, walking way out on glistening stone steps to a rock throne in the middle of our own secret cove, hidden from the top of the cliffs.

You have to get back to shore before the tide comes in and reclaims the throne where you've been sitting.

It won't be in for a few more hours. By then Gabe will have rescued me from this terrible dream I can't stop dreaming.

5

Carolyn Sanders

The news hit school like a bomb. Within seconds, kids were falling apart; boys with their fists in their pockets, scowling; girls clutching one another and sobbing.

For a while they were just milling around in the halls, asking one another, "Did you hear about Gabe?" then repeating the details like a litany.

Gabe was like a god to a lot of these kids. They thought he was indestructible.

I've finally corralled my kids in class. The intercom keeps crackling. The principal is expected to make an address. In the meantime, the kids talk among themselves. Girls' faces are puffy and red.

There's a political struggle in the front office. A group of the teachers want a school assembly, to acknowledge and discuss the accident. The anti-Gabe faction, led by Coach Troy Decker, wants to press ahead with business as usual. We don't want to make him a hero, the coach says.

As if we'll get a damn thing done today. A boy these

17

kids loved has just been killed and I'm supposed to preach the importance of punctuation?

Gabe's brother Gerald was here a while ago, tearing the place apart, looking for James. He burst into my classroom, shouting: "Where the hell is he? He's dead meat!"

James happens to be absent today. With a terrible hangover, no doubt.

I said, "What do you want, Gerald?" I taught him, or attempted to, years ago. Once he actually threatened to hit me. He was suspended for three days.

"I'm looking for James! He killed my brother!"

"Your brother ran off the road," I said, trying not to feel the words I was saying.

"James knows how drunk Gabe gets! He shouldn't have let him drive!" Gerald looked at me sideways, like a dog about to bite.

From the back of the room Ray Jackson spoke up. "James couldn't stop him. Nobody could. Nobody can make Gabe do anything."

"You tell that little sucker he's dead. When I find him—"

"Get out of here, Gerald," I said. "Get out before I call the police."

He killed me with his eyes. Then he slammed out of the room. The kids were frozen at their desks.

"Don't worry," Ray told me. "James can take care of himself."

"Right," I said. "Like Gabe took care of himself." A wave

of despair engulfed me. Gabriel is dead. I saw this coming in his eyes. I saw this coming and I couldn't stop it.

I've heard that Jennie is not in school. Nobody has seen her. At first I was afraid that she'd been in the truck with Gabe, but they said no, Gabe was alone. He was always alone, in the long run.

I wanted to talk to Jennie about Gabe. I wanted to warn her, but it was not my place. I should call her house and see how she's doing, but teacher has no answers today, no words that will take away her pain. Nothing I could say would explain what has happened. It was an accident. If something that deliberate can be called accidental. He threw his life away; batting aside every helping hand, thumbing his nose at every offer of assistance, as if he were entitled to unlimited chances—

Incredible. The kid's dead and I'm still mad at him. He was a splotch on my record, a reminder that I'd failed. The master teacher could not reach him. He shot through life like a falling star. Look, there goes Gabe! we said, dazzled by his brilliance. Then he burned out.

I've been sitting here, reading the pages he wrote for the weekly writing assignment in senior English. He hated that assignment. He didn't trust words. They'd been used to hurt him too many times.

Looking at what he wrote, at that brave, childish scrawl, I can see Gabe's face, I can almost hear him speaking.

6

Gabriel McCloud

Dear Mrs. Sanders,

I don't like this asinement. I don't think its fair. You say just write like your writing to a friend but if you don't I'll flunk you.

That's not to friendly.

I think it should be up to us if we do it or not. I am not the kind of person who likes to write. I don't read much. The stuff I like to read (comix) you would say doesn't count. But some of them are really good I like them a lot. There funny and they tell you stuff about life.

Like this one, this guy's name is SHADOW MAN. He has powers over the weather and the stars and he makes something happen just by thinking it. Mostly he does stuff for good but don't get him pissed off or its tornado time!

I like the way he looks his eyes are like stars I mean they flash. Did you know that when you see a star twinkle its not really happening now it happened a long time ago in the past. It took all that time to get to your eyes because its so far away. That's the kind of thing I learn from this comic and its true.

I don't know what I'm supposed to write. You say write 250 words but I can't its torcher. Anyway its not like people are going to read it just you and its not like I'm going to be a writer or something. We don't have to many books at our house exsept in my mother's room. You can't write at my house its to confusing but that's another story. Anyway my spelling is pretty bad.

282 words! Do I get extra credit?

SHADOW MAN

Gabriel:
Who says you can't write? You're doing it!
Don't worry about spelling and punctuation now. Just get those thoughts on paper.
And no, you don't get extra credit for extra words. Nice try, though. Learning is its own reward. Right? Write!
Keep up the good work.

C.S.

1

David McCloud

Man, this place is a madhouse. What a way to start the day. My brother's dead and my head is killing me. I wish I had some vodka.

The sun's too bright bouncing off the coffee table. We need more curtains. Ma should get some curtains. Jeez, do I feel lousy.

My little brother's dead. I can't believe it. I can't believe he's gone. The first thing I heard is my mother screaming. Five o'clock in the morning. The cops at the door. All the lights go on. I'm lying on the living room couch. Ma's reeling around the room with her hands on her mouth. Frank's pulling on his pants. He almost fell down.

"Are you sure?" he's saying. "How'd it happen?" So then he was supposed to go identify Gabe, like the cops didn't already know he was ours. I kept my eyes closed so I wouldn't have to go. The cops said it wasn't a rush kind of deal.

Ma said she was going. Frank said no, it wasn't something for a woman.

I didn't see what happened next, but it sounded like she spit at him.

Ma went into her room and shut the door. I was lying there thinking. I kept wishing I were dreaming. I wanted to get up and get something to drink, but I didn't want to talk to my father.

After a while they went down to the funeral parlor. Since they got back, Ma hasn't said a word. Not a thing. She's sitting on her bed, just staring, not crying. Gerald went out of here raving like a maniac, saying he was going to kill James. Ma didn't even try to stop him.

When he left, Gerald almost ran over the dog. Frank had tied him up outside because he wouldn't quit barking. He still wouldn't stop. Frank said, "I'm going to shoot him!" So I went out and let Jack loose. He ran down the road, looking for Gabe, I guess.

Oh, man, my head is pounding.

Got to pull myself together and quit doing all this stuff. It's getting me all screwed up. Gabe says—

There's the damn phone again. It won't stop ringing. Everybody's calling. Ma won't come to the phone. Even when it's her own sister. Frank said, "Kat, it's Abby." She still wouldn't take it. He's got to do all the talking.

I wonder who he's talking to now. He's pissed. If this was the old days, he'd rip the phone out of the wall. He's saying, "Yes, yes, I'll be right down," looking lean and mean as a knife. We never called him Dad. He's just our father. Some people call him Francis or Franny.

When I was little I used to think he wasn't my real father 'cause he didn't act like I was his son. People say I look just like him and his dad, my grandpa. I hated that old bastard, but I loved my grandma. She died when I was little. Her name was May June. Her hands were real soft. She smelled like perfume. I can't picture her in my mind anymore, though, and Frank tore up all the pictures one time when he was drunk. But I remember her being huggy and warm and singing me baby songs.

I was trying to pretend I was still asleep, but Frank's standing by the couch, talking to me.

He says, "I have to go down to the police station. Get the phone if it rings."

"What about Ma?"

"What about her?"

"She won't talk."

"She's upset." Frank blows out blue cigarette smoke, which makes him cough, which makes him even madder. But I'm not afraid of Frank anymore. I'm twice as strong as him. The old days are over.

He puts on a jacket. "I'll be back in a while. Clean up that mess."

"What mess?"

He points. "You puked."

Oh, man, what a way to start the day. My baby brother's dead and I'm covered with puke. I've got to get myself together. The problem's not the booze, which I wouldn't need if I didn't have to take the edge off the speed so I can sleep. The problem is I don't have, what do you call it, I don't see myself right. That's the thing. I'm not a bad person. I'm a good person. I could do something big. I need to start over. Clean. I'm not too old, only twenty-five. Twenty-six, I had a birthday last week. Nobody did nothing, no cake or anything, except Gabe gave me a wallet made of genuine leather with a twenty-dollar bill inside. I went down to the Elbow Room and bought everybody drinks.

Too bad I can't check into one of those places where the movie stars go to dry out. Those places cost thousands of bucks. Big money. When you're poor, nobody cares what you do. You could die in the street, they'd sweep you up.

The hell with them. I can make it by myself. That's what Gabe always tells me. I'll do it for Gabe. No booze, no dope. I'll quit smoking too, but not today. There's too much going on now. My brother's dead and my head is killing me. He'll still be dead tomorrow.

I can't believe it. I saw him last night. He was fine, he was laughing and smiling. My baby brother is dead! Where did he go? Is he up in heaven with my grandma? Can you see me, Grammy? Why is life so stupid? Why do all the good people die and the people like Frank live forever?

There's the phone again. I'm all out of smokes. I had a pack. Gerald must've taken them.

Francis McCloud

One good thing was, he didn't look too bad. I was afraid he'd be all messed up. A good-looking boy like Gabriel . . . that would've been hard on his mother.

I didn't want her going down to the funeral parlor, but she just got in the truck and gave me this look like—you'd think I'd killed him. I tried to talk to her, but she wouldn't talk.

At the funeral parlor Morrison rushed out and shook my hand before I could stop him. When I think about him touching my baby boy—

His mother went in to see him first. I thought we should go in together. "I want to see him alone," she said. Her face was like a rock.

She went into this room while I waited in the hall. There was awful music playing and the light was all wrong. I felt like I was underwater.

Katherine let out a scream—it cut right through me. I started to go in there, but Morrison stopped me. He put his hand on my arm and said, "Better wait, Franny," so I sat down and smoked a cigarette.

When Katherine came out she walked right past me and into the parking lot. I heard the truck drive off, but I didn't get mad. The look on her face had spooked me.

"I'll give you a ride home later," Morrison said. "Do you want me to go in there with you?"

I said I didn't. But he'd guessed right; I was afraid to see my own son. Just like at the hospital, when he was born. Kat was propped up in the bed, looking tired but happy, this tiny little face in the crook of her arm. Gabe was a beautiful baby. Even the nurses said so; he was so pretty and peaceful and pink. I stood in the doorway, afraid to go in, shy about laying any claim to him. He looked like something only Katherine had done, like he couldn't have come from me.

Morrison said he'd be right outside if I needed him. I opened the door and walked in. Gabe was on a table across the room, with sheets pulled up to his chin.

His skin was almost glowing and his hair was so bright it looked like light. I pulled off my hat.

I walked over to Gabe and looked down at his face. Suddenly it hit me: This was real, this was happening. My boy was dead. My boy is dead! And this . . . terrible wave rose up in my chest and I thought: Oh, son, how can it all be done? How can it be too late?

My brain felt like it was being ripped out, like a tree

going over in a storm; all the roots ripped up and the wind roaring—I had to get out of that room. I had to leave him.

Morrison wasn't in the hall, but his kid was there. He said to sit down, his dad would be right with me. That kid is such a poor excuse for a man. Soft as a girl, no muscles or balls. I'd be ashamed to have a kid like him. But what can you expect, with a father like that, who milks the dead for a living?

Morrison drove me home. He smelled like soap. His fingers looked like slugs on the steering wheel. "We'll get him ready," he said. "Unless you want him cremated."

"Ready for what?"

"The funeral."

"That's fine, I guess." Things were going too fast. Katherine usually handles stuff like that, anything having to do with the kids.

"Don't worry about it. I'll call you later," he said. "And don't hesitate to ask if you need anything, Franny. You and me go back a long way."

We've despised each other for years. But I saw something new in Morrison's eyes and I realized it was pity. He felt sorry for me, that slimy pervert, with his crazy wife and fairy son. I could've slugged him. Then I remembered about Gabe and I felt so weak, like all my blood was gone.

"Thanks for the ride," I said. "I'll talk to you later." His black Caddy crunched down the road.

David was in the living room, looking real panicked.

He said, "Ma won't talk to me. She just won't talk. Even if you ask her something."

I went down the hall. We have our own rooms. It wasn't my idea.

Katherine was sitting on the edge of her bed. I stood in the doorway. She looked up and saw me. Then she reached out and pushed the door closed.

9

Donald Morrison

Dad worked on Gabriel for a while, and now it looks like Gabe's just sleeping. His cheeks are pink and his eyes are closed. He looks so peaceful.

In a way, that's worse than when they're all torn up, because you look at them and think: Why don't you just wake up and we can make believe none of this happened. I could walk across the room and say, Gabe, wake up, and it would turn out he was only sleeping off a drunk.

Too bad wishes don't come true.

I've been sitting here, looking at him and thinking. I used to wish I were Gabe. It seemed like he had everything. He was really good-looking, and funny too. Everybody liked him, even adults.

He didn't make fun of me like the other kids did. Not that he was a saint. Sometimes he'd smile at the stuff people said ("Donald, you get a lot of stiff ones in that hearse? Haw haw!"), but he wouldn't let them get too mean.

Like that time years ago on the football field. There

was a bunch of kids around me. They were going to pants me. Gabe stopped them.

"What's all this?" he said, walking up, just one of the boys, mildly interested.

"Donald needs some sun. His cheeks are pale," Reynolds said. "He's been lying in a coffin too long."

I remember it was one of those perfect autumn days when you think, Yes, life's worth living. The sky was so blue. Then boys were pulling on me, pushing. I could feel their hot breath. They wanted something to happen.

"Don't you boys have anything better to do?" Gabe didn't sound critical; more like he was just wondering.

"He's a fruit," Reynolds said.

"How do you know?" Gabe asked. "Are you speaking from experience?"

Reynolds looked mad, but he wouldn't fight Gabe. The boys melted away, disappointed.

That meant a lot to me. It wouldn't have been the first time that had happened. Gabe's brother Gerald was in my grade. He threw me out of the locker room naked. I felt like he'd killed me, like I'd died of embarrassment. I didn't go back to school for a week. Once when we were kids he threw dog-doo at me. I said, "You stupid idiot! You got it on your hands!" He wiped them all over my clothes.

People think I'm gay. I'm not. I don't know what I am. I'm almost twenty-one years old and the only females I've ever kissed are my mother and my sister.

When girls find out what I do for a living, they don't want me to touch them. As if death were contagious and could be caught by holding hands. Like this girl I met in Ukiah last summer. We went out a few times: We really liked each other. Then I told her that I help my father. She changed; she looked at me so strangely, as if I'd done something bad. The next time I asked her out, she made excuses. I heard she went away to school.

I am not cut out to be a mortician. So what if it's a family tradition? Does it have to be passed from generation to generation, like a weak chin or heart disease? Once, I said that to my father. He didn't say a word; he just looked at me. The disgust on his face spoke volumes.

My sister Karen thinks he hides his feelings, that he's learned to bury his emotions or he'd go crazy in this job. Because no matter how hard he tries, he can't make his customers happy.

My feeling is, he doesn't have any feelings. Maybe he had some a long time ago, but his father froze them out of him. As his father did to him, as his father did to him. . . . It goes back so far, who do you blame? Maybe I'm the one who'll have to break the chain, so I'll have a chance with my own kids someday, to be all the things that my dad can't be: warm and loving and understanding.

A lot of people are buried with their wedding rings. I wonder if I'll ever get married.

I miss my sister. She's the only person who understands what it's like around here. She ran away from home when she was eighteen, into a lousy marriage. Her husband's a jerk. They're always broke. But she's got two little kids and she feels stuck. My father has never forgiven her for leaving. He says, "She made her own bed. Now let her sleep in it." My mother sends her money on the sly.

I want to leave too, but my mother begs me not to, because then she'd be alone with him. They never kiss or touch. They don't even argue. Why does she stay here? My mother's not crazy. Or maybe she is, I don't know.

I'm worried about Jennie. Gabe's death is going to kill her. Once she told me: I couldn't live without him. That's ridiculous, I said, but she wouldn't listen. When it comes to loving Gabe, she's so stubborn.

I called her house a while ago. "We don't know where she is," her mother said, crying. "She must've heard me on the phone."

We agreed that she probably needs some time alone. Mrs. Harding said she'd give Jennie my message as soon as they found her.

I used to wish I were Gabe. I used to wish he were my brother. Gabe had it all. Now he's got nothing.

I better go splash cold water on my face. My dad would get mad if he caught me crying.

10

Gabriel McCloud

I feel so stupid. I have nothing to say. But I have to write 250 words.

I feel so stupid. I have nothing to say. Let's see that's 28 so far only 222 to go.

Dear Mrs. Sanders,

Hi! How are you! Well, not much is new here so I'll sine off.

Yours Truely,
Gabriel McCloud

You should see the SHADOW MAN comic sometime. I just got the new one. They sell them at the liquor store. That dude is so cool! He looks at people with those big spooky eyes and they lissen! That would come in handy around my house you can't get a word in thier allways screaming. Usally two people so nobody hears what the other ones saying. There just shouting. Its like Madison Swquare Garden there. Just kidding.

I'm at the library now but I have to go soon I'm working part time at the mill. We make coffins and pallets and planter boxes for flowers. My boss sucks but I can use the money my truck guzzles gas and it needs some work but old trucks are still the best.

Thanks for the info about the junior college but after gradation I'm going to work full time at the mill. I can't wait. Not that working at the mill is so great but at least I get payed. School just seems like a waste of time (no offence.) I mean its okay for people like Jennie but I'm not that type I like to work with my hands and stuff. I could maybe work in my dad's body shop but he'd probly drive me crazy.

272 words! That's all folks!

SHADOW MAN

Gabriel:
If you put as much time into your writing as you do into counting words, you could be another Hemingway!
I think the junior college offers classes in auto mechanics.
Interested?

C.S.

11

Jennie Harding

He's dead.

I know he's not coming to get me. There's no use pretending or making up stories. But when I hear the words *Gabriel's dead* inside my head, my mind starts running down this long dark hallway, and all I can think is, No no no, we've got so many plans, we could be so happy—

Dear God, please help me. I am so alone. I am trying to feel you with me. I am trying to feel Gabe's love. The sun is hot, but I cannot stop shaking. I am shaking so hard I could fall off this rock and drown in the ocean and no one would know.

My parents don't want me to go out with Gabe. They think he's a bad influence on me. As if I am a blank wall and Gabe is graffiti. We fight about this all the time.

"He's a very nice boy. We're not saying he isn't. But anyone can see that he's got problems."

By problems, my father means Gabe's family; his blood. The alcoholism and the violence. Mr. McCloud used to get real drunk and beat the boys until he passed out. Sometimes their mother hid them in the woods. She'd hang up a red rag meaning Stay Away. When it was safe to come home, she'd take it down. That's not Gabe's fault. He didn't choose his family. My parents have even tried to bribe me. "We'll send you back east to a wonderful school," they say. "You can stay with Aunt Ruth and Uncle Henry."

They're afraid every time I go out with Gabe, sure that the phone will ring with news that I've died. They're over-protective; I'm their only child. I try to please them, but it's my life.

They must be going crazy with worry. I should have left a note this morning, but what could I have said? *I'm going to meet Gabe.* Where? In heaven? Am I going to kill myself? I couldn't have imagined that before this morning. But I never knew breathing could be so painful, that life could change so much in one second, one day.

Tears are rising from my heart to my throat. If I start, I will never stop crying. My tears will flood the oceans and cover the mountains.

Oh, brother, Gabe would say if he were here.

I must pretend that he is here. I must close my eyes and see him. Nothing bad has happened. He will hold me tight. I can feel him all around me. I love you, Gabe told me; I will love you till the day I die.

Lying on my back, all I see is blank blueness. The sea whispers in my ears. How can I believe that Gabe is up in the sky now when I know he's probably at the funeral parlor, being dressed in the suit he was supposed to wear to high school graduation? We picked it out together. He looked so handsome. Then he decided to drop out. Don't drop out, Gabe! I begged and pleaded. Don't quit school! How can you be so stupid?

He punished me for saying that. He wouldn't see me. I heard that he was going out with Susie Richards. My parents were ecstatic. I was dying inside. But Gabe came back to me; he always comes back. None of this is real. I'm at home in bed, dreaming. Or maybe it's a year from now and this is only a bad memory. Gabe is in bed beside me, holding our baby.

Oh, Gabe, I was so scared, I say. I thought I'd lost you.

You'll never lose me, honey girl. He smiles at me and gently sets the baby on my breast.

Such a beautiful little baby. Still inside me, our secret. Lying here in the sun, I put my hands on my belly and feel the butterfly flutter of the hidden heart. Our son or daughter, sleeping like a seed.

Gabriel would never go away and leave us.

12

James Wilkins

This is the tree that killed Gabe. You can see where the truck hit. The bark's scraped off. There's broken glass all over the ground. Otherwise you'd never know that something bad had happened here.

I had to come see it for myself, to see if I could, I don't know . . . believe what's happened. I mean, I know he's dead. I've seen his truck. But it's like knowing the world's just hanging in space. You can't fit the thought in your head. It's too big.

Ten hours ago we were at Logan's party and I told Gabe, "I'll drive you home."

"The hell you will!" He freaked out. "Get away from me!"

He has this thing about his truck; it's like his wife or something, and nobody else is taking it for a spin.

"Give me the keys, man." I grabbed at his pocket. He whipped around and tried to kick me. People laughed; they thought we were kidding. Most people can't tell when he's wrecked; he hides it. Gabe always had a bad case of pride.

He called me a few choice names and split. It didn't mean nothing; we've had worse fights than that. Gabe's been my best friend since second grade.

When I got to school this morning and they told me what had happened, I had to leave right away, I felt sick. It felt like the top of my head was blown off and my brain was a cold wind.

People called me at home and said: You better lay low. Gerald's looking for you.

Like I'm shaking in my boots. Like I'm scared to death. I know Gerald, I know how dirty he fights. It's hilarious, him acting like this is all my fault and he's going to kill me for killing his brother. When the fact is, he hates Gabe, he's jealous of him, because everybody loves Gabe and everybody hates Gerald because Gerald is a low-down dirty dog.

I hope he finds me. I'm ready for him. I feel like hitting something. Hard.

They say the funeral's on Monday. Gabe would hate that, lying there while everybody stares at him. He wants his ashes thrown off a cliff into the ocean. We were talking about that one time. Actually, he didn't say ashes; he said throw his body out the back of his pickup. And he wants it at sunset, with the sky all bloody, and one of those— what do you call them?—bagpipes playing. Gabe's Scotch and he likes the sound of those things. To me it sounds like something being strangled.

But he won't get no ocean or bagpipes. All he's going

to get is the funeral parlor, and those geeks are going to make him look like someone I never knew. I went by there on my way here and they wouldn't let me see him. They said he wasn't ready. Like he was going on a date or something! He's dead! What the hell do I care what he looks like? He's practically my brother. I've seen Gabe every which way there is; naked and laughing, and sick and drunk, in a blue tuxedo, and with his mouth bashed in, so there's no way he could look that would blow my mind. Except for how he'll look when they get through with him.

I'm supposed to work Monday afternoon. If I go to the funeral, that butthook will dock me or say I might lose my job. So what. I hate that place. Gabe got me on there. He's the only thing that keeps me going because he jokes about it and flips off the boss.

Gabe's going to be planted in one of those coffins. Wouldn't it be weird if he or I had made it, and someone had come up to us that day and said, Guess who's going to end up in this box!

No way, we would've said. No way that's going to happen.

I don't care if I get fired, 'cause I'm leaving town. Maybe go to Reno or San Francisco. I've been working on my Harley, getting it all fixed up, almost like I knew this trip was coming. I'm not taking anything with me, 'cause there's nothing to take; nothing I can't find someplace else. Except Gabe, and now he's gone. Oh, man, it's so crazy. I'm standing here looking at the glass on the ground, sticking my fingers in this gashed-up tree. Too bad I'm not one of those TV preachers. I'd call out: Lord, please heal this tree! And time would go backward and the bark would jump on, and Gabe's truck would fly down the road in reverse, all the way back to Logan's party. It would be different this time. Gabe wouldn't get so drunk. Neither would I. I'd trick him into giving me the keys. He'd be mad as hell when it was time to leave, but I wouldn't care; he'd still be alive.

If only we'd left sooner. If only we hadn't gone. I keep going over the whole thing in my mind, trying to figure out how it couldn't have happened, and this whole stupid thing is just something I imagined. But that broken glass keeps winking at me.

13

Gerald McCloud

I went downtown a while ago and looked at Gabe.
They're getting him all fixed up, with his hair combed
wrong and makeup on him. He didn't look too happy. He
used to always be laughing, like life was some big comedy
show.

Looks like the joke's on you, little brother.

Seemed funny to see him lying there, helpless. With
not even the strength to raise his head. Who knows what
those faggots have been doing to him. I cornered fatso
Donny and said, "Keep your hands off my brother, fruit."
His eyes were all wet and red.

Nobody's ever going to get their hands on me. When
the party's over, I'm gone. Think I'll stick around and get
old like Frank? I hated him, but I was proud of his strength.
If he couldn't fix something, he'd break it. He'd tear that
sucker apart. A lamp or a transmission, you name it. Especially when he was hitting the sauce.

He stopped drinking two years ago when he almost
killed Gabe; pulled a gun on him right there in the kitchen.

He'll probably start again. Gabe was always his favorite. Everybody always likes Gabe the best. Even Jerry Dean. I could tell by the way she looked at him. Dancing with him that night at the bar. She made me look like a fool. I straightened her out later. I didn't hit her that hard; her teeth were already loose. All she eats is Coke and candy. Anyway, I wouldn't have had to hit her in the first place if she hadn't been acting like a slut.

I went by there this morning and she said, "You must be happy now!" and slammed the door in my face. That bitch. Everybody always feels sorry for Gabe, like he's the only one that matters. I'll tell you something: He had it good. By the time the old man got to him, he'd worn himself out on me and David.

I saw Frank kill a cat when I was little. Threw it into the wall and broke its neck. And he shot this puppy right in front of me and David 'cause when he called the puppy, it ran to David. David cried, but I didn't. No tears from me. I wouldn't give the old man nothing.

He made me tough. That's the one thing he done for me. Nothing can hurt me, or if it does, I'll hurt it right back and make it stick.

Wait till I get my hands on James. I'll keep driving around till I find him. Thinks he can mess with my family like that. He should've drove Gabe home. He should see my mother. I'd like to drag him over there and say: Look at her face! She won't talk to me, you bastard! She's never going to be the same again!

Nothing will ever be the same. That stupid Gabe can't hold his liquor. Give him a few drinks and he acts like a fool. He's just like David. I can take it or leave it. Booze ain't the only way to get high. Pills are better. If the cops stop you, you can swallow the evidence. I sat in jail one time on ten tabs of acid and a bunch of speed and nobody could tell. Frank came down there and bailed me out, then we get outside and he acts like he's going to slug me. So I gave him a little tap to remind him: I ain't a kid anymore. I want respect.

The only person I can really count on is my mother. Or I could before this happened. I mean, I always knew she loved Gabe the most, because he was the baby and everybody made a big fuss about him. But my mom always acted like she loves me too. Now she don't say nothing. She just stares straight ahead, and when I ask her something, she looks like she don't even know me.

I'm going to tell James: You didn't just kill Gabe. She's dead. You killed my mother. I'm going to make him pay for all the damage he's done. People think they can mess with you and walk away.

James won't be walking when I'm through with him.

14

Carolyn Sanders

Maybe this assembly will calm the kids down. Gabe's death has burst their protective bubble. If he can die, it can happen to them. No wonder they're so sad and angry.

The school nurse is talking to them about drinking and driving. Beth means well, but she oversimplifies; she makes alcohol sound like a splinter. Pluck it out and the problem's all gone. Unless you're an alcoholic like Gabe. Most people didn't see him that way. They thought he just drank a lot of beer, like half the senior class.

The coach is glaring at me from the back of the hall. Decker was dead set against this assembly. We got into a screaming match in the principal's office. He said, "You're trying to make a hero out of a cheap little punk!" I could've punched him.

I said, "Gabe wasn't a hero and he wasn't a punk. He was a hometown boy and these kids loved him. You didn't like him because you couldn't make him jump."

The coach hates my guts too. He thinks I'm a bleeding heart liberal. He thinks talking about feelings and problems is stupid. Got a problem? Here, bite on this bullet. He'd had trouble with Gabe's brothers and holds a grudge.

My introduction to Gabe was in freshman English. I thought he'd be like David and Gerald, whose idea of making their marks was carving their names into desk tops.

Gabe was different. He was funny and bright. He spoke up in class and liked to make people laugh. Which was classic, because his home life was so tragic. Over the years, I've met with his parents several times. I preferred talking to his mother, although she'd always defend him. You couldn't have a discussion with Francis; you'd have a fight. He thought that school was a waste of time and that I was a prime offender.

I've just asked the kids to share some memories of Gabe. Hands are waving in the air. "I remember the time Gabe," Ray Jackson begins, and all the girls are smiling and crying.

The more people talk, the worse I feel, as if all those words were landing on my chest. I can feel the kids watching me. They know I'm upset. That scares them. They want me to tell them that everything will be all right. In class I had them write down their feelings. One of them asked me, "Does spelling count?"

Not for much. "Not today," I said.

After ninth grade, I didn't have Gabe again until this year. At first he seemed to enjoy the class. I helped him with his reading and writing. He had some kind of a learning disability, so I recommended testing. "There's nothing wrong with me," he said. His parents never responded to the letters I sent them.

He was smart enough to realize he was wasting his life and not smart enough—or strong enough—to change. Gabe had so much potential. That drives teachers crazy. We all hope we're inspiring the next Curie or Einstein. We can hear the Nobel Prize acceptance speech: "I want to thank my teacher. . . ." I knew Gabe was special, and he liked that I knew that, and he hated it too. He hated me for pointing out the difference between who he could be and who he was.

If I'd said that to him, he would've laughed in my face. He would've claimed he didn't know what I meant.

One night, not long ago, he came by my house, so drunk I didn't know him, lost and raging. He told me to stop encouraging Jennie to go to college. He clearly feared that if she went, he'd lose her. I mentioned this and he called me a liar. Before he left, he said some awful things. I wouldn't have recognized myself from his description.

Now the principal, Dick Peterson, is telling the kids that Gabe would want us to carry on; that he'd want us to go back to class and work hard.

A reporter from the *Ukiah Daily Journal* called me this morning. He was interviewing some of Gabe's teachers. He asked if I thought Gabriel's death was a suicide. A large percentage of teenage traffic fatalities are subconsciously intentional, the reporter confided.

I told him Gabe's death wasn't a suicide; but who's to

say? If you asked Gabe, he'd deny it. It's not like he took a gun and blew his brains out. It's more like he turned his back on life and walked away. Some kids are like that. You can't reach them, but there's something about them that makes you keep trying. It's like going after a drowning man who keeps swimming toward the horizon.

15

Gabriel McCloud

Guess who? That's right yours truely with another thrilling story of life in the fast lane Starring SHADOW MAN!!!

One thing about him he doesn't have any family getting in his hair all the time. See he was rasied on this distant planet and then he came to Earth and left them all behind. The people who rasied him did it right they taut him what he needs to know to survive. When he was just a baby they taut him to be tough like when he was cold his mother carved him a coat of ice and said "Put this on and draw warmth from it and you'll never have to fear the cold." So he did. And when he was to hot because the sun was so close his father held him over a fire and said "Take the heat inside your bones and you'll never be burned" and so he wasn't. And when he was thirsty and wanted some milk his mother took a knife and cut Shadow Man's wrist and said "Drink yourself and you'll never be thirsty" or something like that and so he wasn't. And when he was hungry and wanted some food his dad gave him a stone and said "Eat this it will sharpen your teeth and if you can eat stones you'll never go hungry." So he's not exsactly your average guy but it gives him the strength to fight evil (live spelled backward.) Not that he goes around like Superman or something that guy is such a wimp.

Nobody tells Shadow Man what to do he decides what to do and does it. He can read people's minds and he knows what thier thinking and he helps a lot of people out of trouble.

If I was Shadow Man I'd change a lot of things like the way people treat Manuel. Its not his falt he's Mexican. That's how he is. People make fun of him when he talks in class because he has that aksent but at least he's trying. That's more then some people. I told James to shut up and leave him alone and we got in a big fight. (Ya! I won!) It isn't right what Manuel has to put up with then I think well he might as well get used to it that's life. You either get tough or you die.

Well I've gone way over my limit lots of words this time so next time I don't have to write so many right?

SHADOW MAN

Gabe:
Wrong. Keep up the good work. You're doing beautifully!
P.S. I think it's great that you're speaking up for Manuel.
The other kids look up to you, Gabe. They really do. Set them
a good example.

C.S.

16

Jennie Harding

It is so quiet here. There is no sound. Even the waves are silent; as if I were lying on the bottom of the ocean, the water above me as blue as the sky, the gulls flashing by like fish.

I am suspended in stillness, on the crest of the wave, in the breathless hush just before the wish. I have pushed back the world. I have made a safe place for my baby and me.

If I try very hard and hold my mind tight, I can keep out the terrible pictures: the crying faces, the open mouths. The sea is motionless. Time is my prisoner. I have carved out a moment that does not exist; it's now and no tomorrow.

And I see my lover, rising like the sun, then bending to kiss me, his breath a warm breeze, his blue eyes deep enough to drown my fear.

The rock is hot, but the water is cool. I dangle my toes. Waves come nibbling like fish. I feel Gabriel pressing kisses on my lips, his tongue as sweet as chocolate.

Put your hands on my belly. Can you feel the baby, swimming in the dark like a minnow? We don't even know who's in there, you said. Yes, we do, I said; it's you and me.

The walls of my mind are stretching, shrieking. Hold on tight. Got to hold on tight. Imagine Gabriel's face above me. Inches away. He is kissing my throat.

I have to use all my strength to hold this moment in place, to make a space for Gabriel and the baby and me. Together forever. I can't keep out the sound. The roaring and pounding. Gabe is slipping away. *Don't leave me!*

Clouds are gathering. Waves are crashing. The storm is coming. Can you hear the thunder? My God, it sounds like Gabriel's truck, hitting and hitting and hitting that tree, over and over, until nothing is left.

Not even me.

17

Joey Hammer

I ran into Franny coming out of the liquor store. He looked terrible.

"How you doing?" I asked, a stupid question. But what was there to say?

"Pretty bad." He looked at me sideways. That's his way.

"I'm awful sorry about Gabe," I said. Franny cracked open a fresh pack of Salems. He might've bought a bottle too, but that's his business. What's the point of staying sober now? So he can tell how bad he's feeling?

People are saying this is a punishment from God, for all of Franny's sins.

The hell it is. Fran's been punished enough. Anyhow, God wouldn't use Gabe that way. Gabe's just a kid, he didn't do nothing wrong.

"How's Katherine taking it?" We were standing outside, leaning against the wall by the newspaper racks.

"Not too good," Franny said. "The minister just left. She wouldn't talk to him."

"She must be pretty upset."

"She hasn't said one word since she saw Gabe this morning." Fran's face was the color of the newspapers.

"There anything I can do?" I started to reach out my hand, but he's not the kind of guy you touch.

He shook his head. "Gabe's girlfriend took off. Nobody's seen her all morning. Her father called the house. He's been looking. Guess I'll drive around and keep my eyes open."

"What about Katherine?"

"She wants to be alone. Anyway, David's there with her."

"You want some company?"

"No," he said. "I mean, thanks anyway."

"Maybe I'll drive around too," I told him. "Did she and Gabe have a place they liked to go, someplace in particular?"

"Not that I know of." He rubbed his eyes. Franny looked like he hadn't slept in a week and might never sleep again.

I got in my car and started driving. There's way too much country to cover. I didn't see Jennie. All I saw was Franny's face and those sad eyes behind his glasses.

He was real good-looking when he was young. And Kat was so pretty. They were the perfect couple. And hungry for each other. You could see it in their eyes. Like they couldn't wait to be alone.

We'd be over there a lot, years ago, playing cards, a bunch of us young married couples. Sometimes Fran would get out his guitar. We used to say he was the next Hank Williams.

That first baby they had, he was really something. Francis Timothy. They called him Timmy. Golden-haired and pink-cheeked. We teased Kat about that, 'cause she and Franny were dark. Sweet little boy. His daddy was so proud of him. Bought him his own little toy guitar. Couldn't wait to take him hunting and fishing.

A bunch of us boys were there the night it happened, playing cards and drinking beer. Katherine had walked down the road to some baby shower one of the gals was having. The little boy was sleeping in his crib. It was a real pretty night. The sun was going down, the sky was silver.

The next thing we know, we hear this terrible noise around front, where there's this little pond that Franny stocked with catfish. When we get there, Katherine's standing in it, screaming, holding up her dead baby boy.

It wasn't nobody's fault. He'd got out of his crib. But Katherine blamed Franny. She never forgave him. Sometimes I think she stayed with him all these years just to hate him. At the time it happened, she was pregnant with David, then the other ones came along. When Gabe was a baby he looked like Timmy. The other boys take after Fran.

It wasn't his fault. He wasn't drunk that night. Ask anybody who was there. It was one of those things. It was life, it could happen to anyone.

I drove around for an hour with no sign of Jennie, but I did see Gabe's dog. He was heading toward the highway. He stopped when I called him, but then he took off.

I wish there was something I could do for Fran. He seems real tough, but this has broken his heart. And Katherine not talking. Somebody's got to do something. Unfortunately, they ain't running over with friends. I asked my wife to go talk to Kat, but she wouldn't; she was too scared.

I saw Tom Dawson coming out of the post office. I pulled over, but he wouldn't come up to the car.

"You hear about Gabe?" I asked. I figured he had.

He nodded. "I went out there."

"To the house?"

"To the wreck." He wanted to get away, but I wouldn't let him.

"I ran into Franny at the liquor store," I said.

He looked real scornful. "That figures."

"He was buying cigarettes. Anyway, who could blame him if he took a drink now?"

Tom shrugged and edged toward his car.

"Franny says Katherine won't talk," I said.

That got his attention. He stopped walking.

"Won't talk?" he said.

"She's too upset. You've got to go over there, Tom."

He shook his head. "That's got nothing to do with me."

"I know how you feel, but that's the past," I said. "This ain't the time to hold a grudge. For God's sake, Tom, she's your sister."

18

Tom Dawson

I wasn't sorry she married him. I grew up with Franny.
If anyone could handle him, it was Katherine. They'd gone
together forever, so there wasn't any question that they'd
get married.

Fran was slick, he was a wheeler-dealer. He always had
a piece of every game in town. He'd show up with something brand-new and expensive—a shotgun, a chain saw,
a truck, for God's sake, and you had to wonder: Was it
hot?

None of that mattered to Katherine. The shadows
added to his charm. He was handsome and smart, and he
could make people laugh.

It's hard to picture that Franny now.

Of course, he could turn on you in a minute, with a
wit that cut like a knife. Sense your weak spot and shove
the blade in it. When he was drinking, he fought all the
time. He'd kick, bite, whatever it took, even jump you from
behind. He left me alone because I was bigger than he was

and in those days I had a bad temper. Now things make me sad instead of mad. It's no improvement.

Years ago we were over there a lot, Kay and me, playing cards. I was there the night the baby died. Katherine blamed Franny, but she wouldn't leave him, she wouldn't leave him no matter how bad things got. It was like they were locked in a fight to the finish and neither one was going to cry uncle.

The boys were a mess. Look at David and Gerald. I'm ashamed to admit they're my flesh and blood. Gabe was the only one—what's the use? I had to pry him out of that truck, his blood on my hands, my sister's blood. I feel like smashing all the windows in this store. Customers come in and pretend to shop. They buy nails or a package of sandpaper. But what they really want is the gory details: Did Gabe go through the windshield? Was his head cut off? As if the truth weren't bad enough.

Becky's offered to go over and see Katherine, but it's not her responsibility. It's been eight years since I set foot in that house. Ever since the car deal. Fran shafted me.

I called the twins to tell them that their cousin is dead. Randy said, "Dad, you've got to go over there. You have to forgive and forget."

I can't. That house is so full of hate that you can feel it when you walk through the door. Why do people want to live like that? Katherine and Franny should've gone their separate ways. It was different in the old days. Before Timmy died. They were happy. Fran was making good money in construction and quite a bit on the side. He bought that Chevy pickup, the one he's still driving. He even wears his hair like he did back then, too long for a man his age.

I've picked up the phone a couple of times. I even started dialing. But it's been too long. There's too much to say. And nothing to say at all.

19

Gerald McCloud

I can't find James. He must be hiding. I stopped by the Lockhorn for a quick snort. Inside, it was as dark as a cave.

I sat at the bar. Everybody was watching me. Then I said, "Anybody seen James?"

If they had, they weren't saying. Bunch of old losers, sitting around getting tanked all day. One old boy—Fritz— said, "Better go home, Gerald, before you get yourself in trouble."

"What kind of trouble?" I gave him the look Frank used to give us just before he started swinging.

Fritz looked so scared I almost laughed. He stared down inside his drink, mumbling.

The bartender, a fat broad, says to me, "We don't want no trouble here."

"I was just asking Fritz what kind of trouble did he mean! In case you haven't heard, my brother's dead!"

"Have another drink, Gerald," Fritz said. "On me."

"I don't want another drink! I want to find James! That bastard killed my brother!"

Susie Richards was down at the end of the bar. She's thin and witchy with long twitchy legs. I used to picture them wrapped around me. Then Gabe came along and screwed that up.

"I'll buy you a drink," I said to her.

"Hell, no." She stuck another cigarette in her mouth. I used to picture putting my mouth on her mouth and kissing her so hard she couldn't talk.

That ticked me off, but I didn't show it. "I know how you feel," I told her.

"No, you don't," she said. "I'm glad he's dead. Now he's dead for everybody, not just me. Comes around acting like he loves me so much, then dumps me like I don't mean nothing. The hell with him. The hell with you!" She'd been holding down that barstool for a while.

"Maybe we could go for a ride," I said. "I'm looking for James. You could help me."

"What good's that going to do?" she said. "It's not his fault your brother couldn't hold his liquor. Besides"—she looked right in my face—"I wouldn't ride with you if you was the last man in the world. You can go straight to the devil."

I started toward her.

"Hold it, Gerald." The bartender opened a drawer that I happen to know holds a gun.

I said, "That bitch better quit bad-mouthing my brother!" Everybody was staring at me. I knocked over some chairs on my way out.

He's dead and he's still getting me in trouble. We got in a big fight last week. He walked in while I was slapping David around. I work hard for my money and David always takes it, getting in my wallet and my dresser drawers. He blows it on booze and buying drinks for everybody, playing the big man at the Elbow Room and the Lockhorn. Let him work for a living. It don't grow on trees. I sell firewood, meth, abalone out of season. Anyway, I wasn't hitting him hard; I was just making a point.

Gabe runs into the living room and jumps over the couch like he's Superman or something. He's always showing off.

"What the hell are you doing?" he says.

I let go of David. He slumped on the floor, blubbering. It was just a big show; he was too drunk to feel a thing.

"Butt out," I said. "This is none of your business."

David said something, but you couldn't tell what; the words were all slobbered up.

"He steals my money and gets drunk," I said.

"I don't care what he does. Don't hit him," Gabe said.

"Who's going to stop me?"

"I am." Gabe's chest was all puffed up. He thinks he's really something.

"Just run along and play with your girlfriend," I said. "From what I hear, she don't put out. I guess that's why you keep Susie on the side."

I knew that would get him. He said, "Shut your dirty mouth!"

"I hope Jennie don't find out," I said. "That would break her little heart."

It was almost a relief when we started punching, like our hands was finally doing the talking. David was lying on the floor, hollering. Then like magic a knife was in my hands. Gabe saw it and started laughing, like it wasn't for real, like I was some big joke. I wanted to rip his smile wide open. David was yelling, "Gerald, don't!"

Then Ma was in the room. She threw groceries at me, out of a paper bag she was holding. She kept hitting me with a long loaf of bread. You wouldn't think bread would be that hard.

"Stop it, stop it, stop it!" she said. "Get out of here and don't come back! All of you! Go ahead and kill each other! Just leave me alone!"

She went into her room and slammed and locked the door. Gabe knocked and knocked, but she wouldn't answer.

So I left the house and drove around. Sometimes it seems like I live in this truck. Like it's the only place that's really mine. I listen to the radio. I hate the talk shows. People blabbing on and on.

I find some song I like and crank up the volume until the music's screaming in my mind. The windshield's rattling and the steering wheel's shaking, I go faster and faster, and it's like anything could happen, the truck could blow up or the world could explode.

20

David McCloud

All hell's broke loose. It turns out Jennie's pregnant. Her father was over here, almost busted down the door. You'd think we had something to do with it.

I said, "My father's not here. You better come back later."

Mr. Harding's face was red. "He's probably down at the bar!"

"You better quit yelling. My mother's real upset."

"My daughter's five months pregnant!" he shouted. "We've got to find her!"

He thinks she's going to kill herself because she's pregnant. Turns out her mother went into her room, looking for a clue to where Jennie might be, found her diary and read it.

I said, "It seems kind of funny you never noticed she was pregnant."

"Not with the clothes the kids wear today! Big baggy things! She didn't want us to find out!"

"You don't need to get so mad about it."

"Don't tell me what to do! I could sue you McClouds!"

"Go ahead," I said. "Go on down to Morrison's and sue my brother, for all the good it'll do you."

I felt sorry for him, but it wasn't my fault. I get tired of people yelling at me.

He said, "In her diary she mentions some place she and Gabe always went, somewhere on the coast. Do you know where it is?"

"No, he never said."

"Well, you better start looking!"

"There's a hundred miles of beach around here!"

"I don't care if it's a million!" He was spitting, he was so mad. "We've got to find her!"

"I've got to stay here with my mother."

"I should've known you people wouldn't give a damn!" Mr. Harding tore up the driveway, pulling out.

I thought Ma might come to see what was going on. But if she'd heard about the baby, she didn't let on. The door to her room stayed closed.

Gerald called a while ago to see how Ma was doing.

"The same," I said. "Why don't you come home?" If he talked to her, she might say something.

"No," he said. "I'm looking for James."

"What for?" I said. "That won't do any good." But he hung up.

I felt so bad I went out to pet Jack; then I remembered I'd let him off his rope.

Frank came back to check on Ma. I told him about

Jennie's baby. "That stupid kid," he said. Which one did he mean? Probably all of them. He went down the hall and opened my mother's door and told her the situation.

He said, "She and Gabe had some special place, on the coast somewhere. Do you know it?"

I could hear her not answering. I could feel her staring at him.

He said, "Damn it, Katherine, he was my son too!"

He came back into the living room. I told him Morrison had called. He said to go down there and see what Morrison wanted. Money, probably, or maybe he needed to know some stuff, like how do we want the funeral. I told Frank he should go down there himself because Morrison sounded like he was in a hurry. That made Frank really mad.

"What's the rush?" he roared. "Gabe's not going anywhere! You tell that bastard—" A bunch of stuff. Then he left. So I have to go down there. I don't want to go. I've never been around a dead person before, especially my brother. I hope Morrison don't ask me if I want to see him, 'cause I don't. Anyway, that body ain't really Gabe. It's like the shell on something or the husk on corn, or like dropping your dirty clothes on the floor and stepping into something brand-new. I hope so. Or maybe it's like nothing at all.

I wish Uncle Tom would call so I could ask him to go with me. You'd think he would; we're family. But he acts like we all died years ago and he don't even see us. That's not right. Ma loves him, but she'd never call him, not after the things he said. She knows he was right, at least about that car, but he shouldn't have said all that other stuff. It just hurt everybody's feelings.

I better tell Ma I'm going, even though she don't care. I hate going in there. She's acting so spooky.

"Ma?" She's sitting on the edge of her bed, her feet on the floor, her eyes straight ahead, looking at me like I'm a stranger, like I'm selling something she don't need.

"Mama, I'm going down to the funeral parlor, to see about Gabe."

I hear what I'm saying. The words explode inside my head. I'm dying, my brain is bleeding.

"Oh, Mama! Gabe's dead! I'm sorry, Mama!" I'm down on my knees, my head in her lap. "Oh, Mama! I'm sorry! I'm sorry! Please, Mama!" I can't stop crying. I hurt so bad. "Why's he dead? I'm sorry, Mama!"

Her hand comes down and strokes my head.

21

Gabriel McCloud

Dear Mrs. Sanders,

I really didn't like what you said in class that stuff about the trees and the loggers. You don't know much about it just because your a teacher doesn't give you the right to tell people what to think. That's not fair.

The problem is these damn stupid tree lovers who think trees and birds are more important than people. They've really screwed things up. What are the loggers suppose to do? That's the only job they ever had. Now you say well that's too bad they'll have to do something else. Like what? Thats all they know. At the mill where I work if they don't get the wood the people will be layed off and lots of them have familys. Its not like they can be brain surgens or something they work with there hands that's what they do. Like my brother David he worked in the mill pulling green chain till he hurt his back. Then they let him go and didn't give him nothing. They don't care about us they just want the money and he can't even get disability.

Look in the woods there's plenty of trees. You probly think I'm rude but it makes me mad. These people come up from the city and tell us what to do a bunch of hippys they don't even work. Me and James got into it with some people in Ukiah last week. They were standing around with sines Save The Forest Stop The Logging stuff like that. This one guy had real long hair and James tore up his sine then the cops came but we didn't get in trouble.

We went over there to get the new Shadow Man. The liquer store here didn't get thier shipment. So we went over there and go in this store and the guy acts like were going to rob the place. That allways happens to teenagers. The new issue is great Shadow Man wipes out this gang all by himself and everybodys glad because they were selling drugs to kids. Shadow Man helps kids he says the're to little to help themselfs. To bad these people who want to save the trees don't care about the kids instead.

So anyway I hope you don't think I'm ragging on you its just that if it wasn't for the loggers you wouldn't have a house or planter boxes or things like that. Yours Truely,

SHADOW MAN

71

Gabriel:

I'm sorry you were offended by my remarks in class. But the trees have been cut down too fast for years. What will happen to the loggers when the trees are gone?

We all need to plan ahead. Even you. Have you given any thought to the junior college?

C.S.

22

Francis McCloud

I figured I might as well look for Jennie. It was obvious
Katherine didn't want me around. Even with her door shut
I could feel her staring at me. So I got in the truck and
started driving.

Katherine's never going to smile at me again. There
was always the chance things might change. Now they
won't. She'll always be sad. Gabe will always be dead. This
is just the kind of stupid world that would take him and
leave David.

I know it's a sin to wish your own son dead, but when
I see him around town, stumbling and mumbling, it makes
me feel like a failure. Like God's laughing at me, saying,
See what you done? He should talk. He left his own son
on the cross. Jesus died for our sins, but the world's still
a mess. He wrestled the devil and lost.

I swear to God I'm losing my mind.

I wish Jennie would turn up. Her folks are scared. A
nice girl like her, she wouldn't do nothing crazy. But kids
are funny; they feel stuff so strong. She looks at Gabriel

like he's so great. That's how Katherine used to look at me, before everything got screwed up. Now her eyes are like bullets. What does she want from me? Haven't I supported her all these years, given her a home and a family? Why does she hate me?

That's what I was asking her two years ago, the night I finally gave up the bottle. The boys were out, and me and Kat were alone. I wanted to be close. I'd been drinking. So had she. We started yelling at each other and knocking stuff over. Then everything went topsy-turvy.

Katherine got hurt. I'm not sure how. She was down on the floor and her nose was bleeding. Then Gabe was in the room. He threw me into the wall. "Don't touch her! Don't you dare hurt her!" he's screaming. He didn't even know what was going on, but I was too far gone to explain that Katherine was the one who had started it; when I tried to kiss her, she bit me.

I went into the bedroom and got my rifle and went back into the kitchen. Gabe was bending over his ma. She screamed when she saw me. He didn't look scared. He said, "Go ahead and shoot me, you crazy old fart! You've already killed everybody in this house!"

I almost pulled the trigger. But suddenly I saw him; I saw that I was going to shoot my own son. I ran outside and threw the gun in the pond. I haven't touched a drop since that night, not even a single shot. Because I'd rather be dead than hurt my own children. Katherine thinks it's my fault Timmy died, but it's not. I was just playing cards.

He climbed out of his crib. I would've cut off my arm if it would've brought him back, but wishing and crying don't change a damn thing.

This driving around is getting me no place. Jennie won't be found till she wants to be found. That's the thing about kids; they're so selfish. They don't think about other people's feelings.

I've got a bottle with me now, in the glove compartment. Picked it up this morning, just in case. In case the pain gets too bad. Like in the Civil War. Somebody got hurt, they'd give him whiskey, if they had it, and operate on him right there in the field. Cut off the hurt part, an arm or a leg. Most of them didn't make it.

I vowed on my son's life that I wasn't going to drink. But it didn't do no good. He's just as dead now as if I'd shot him.

23

Jennie Harding

We'd done a lot of things, we'd kissed and touched, but we hadn't made love, not all the way. Gabe wanted to. "Why not?" he'd say. "Don't you really love me?"

He knew I did. But no matter how much love I gave him, he was starving. He never understood why people loved him. He thought it was some kind of trick.

I was afraid to make love. I didn't want to take chances. "It's not like I'm going to get you pregnant," he said. We argued about that. We argued a lot. He absolutely didn't want me to go away to college.

We had an awful fight about that, one night, here on the beach. We'd been wrapped in blankets, looking at the stars, just talking. Then I told him about this brochure I'd received, from a college back east. Gabe went crazy. He was screaming that it was Mrs. Sanders's fault; that she thought I was too good for him. "Oh, you're such a brain," he sneered. "Much too good for Willow Creek."

He kept ranting and raving. He wouldn't listen to me.

This time I didn't feel like apologizing. I felt cold and hard inside. I got up and started walking.

"Where do you think you're going?" he called.

"Back to town," I said. "I've had it."

He came after me. He tried to make me stop walking. "Jennie, I'm sorry. Honey girl, please listen—"

"I'm not listening to you anymore!" I said. "You say you love me, then you treat me like this! You say you won't drink—I smell beer on your breath! Mrs. Sanders doesn't hate you; you hate yourself! If you want to wreck your life, go ahead! But leave me alone!"

I hadn't talked like that to Gabriel before. He looked shocked. He burst into tears. He was like a little boy, clinging to me, pleading. "Please don't go!" he sobbed. "Please don't leave me!"

I had never seen Gabe cry. He'd rather shed blood than tears. I was crying too. We sat down on the sand. We kissed and hugged. I wanted to be inside him, to fill up all the places that were sad and empty.

It was just that once. It only happened one time. When my period was late, I could not believe it. It took me months to accept that the baby was real and not a figment of my guilty imagination.

Sometimes I've wondered if Gabe wanted to make me pregnant, so I couldn't escape, so I wouldn't leave him.

I don't believe that abortion is a sin and that people who do it will go to hell. Gabriel thinks people should have to have kids, even when they don't want them. He doesn't like women having so much power, or that a decision like that could be up to me.

We were here, on the rock, when I told him I was pregnant. Things had gotten bad; we were always fighting. I had made up my mind to tell him we were through. He'd gotten so strange. He was drinking all the time. When I asked him about it, he'd deny it. He couldn't have fun unless he was high. Those were the only times he told me he loved me.

I didn't love Gabriel any less. It was just that I'd realized that he wasn't going to change. He wasn't going to stop drinking, or fighting, or sneaking around seeing other girls. He thought I didn't know about that. As if you could keep a secret in Willow Creek.

When I told him about the baby, he looked both scared and pleased. His eyes flashed more thoughts than I could read. Then his face hardened, shutting me out.

"What're you going to do about it?" he asked, as if the whole thing was my responsibility.

"Get an abortion," I said. "It's already scheduled." I was afraid to make the appointment, but I'd done it, feeling like I was someone else, like I didn't know myself anymore.

I told him I thought we should break up, or at least stop seeing each other for a while.

Gabe looked stunned. He almost hit me. He stood above me, blocking the sun. The shadow of his hand landed on my face. When I didn't flinch, he broke down.

He said, "I promise I'll change! This time I mean it! Things are going to be different! Just wait and see. Give me one more chance. Don't kill the baby! I'll be good to you, honey! Jennie, please don't leave me!"

His sadness overwhelmed me. I loved him so much. I thought the power of my love could overcome all our problems.

I was so stupid.

I haven't told my parents about the baby. Whenever I try, the words dry up in my throat. I keep picturing how those words will change my mother's face. So I've waited and waited, as if the baby might disappear. . . . Now it's too late to undo what's been done. I'm caught in the present and Gabe has escaped. He didn't want the baby; he wanted me.

My belly is swelling, even my face is changing. My parents would've found out soon, when they finally saw what they didn't want to see. They would've been mortified, angry, hurt. How could you do this to us? they would say, as if I were only a mirror for their dreams.

It would hurt them most to know that this had nothing to do with them. That night on the beach they didn't even exist. The whole world was Gabe and me.

24

Donald Morrison

The oldest brother, David, came down here to settle some business for his father. I asked him if he wanted to look at Gabe.

He shook his head no. His hands were trembling.

"I'll go in there with you, if you want me to," I said. His eyes are as big as Gabe's, but dark.

He glanced toward the parking lot, then back at the door to the room that holds Gabe's body.

"All right," he said. He stayed close by me. He smelled of booze and cigarettes.

Five feet from the worktable, David stopped walking. "I can't," he said.

"He looks okay," I said. "It just looks like he's sleeping."

"But he's not." David reached for a cigarette, then put the pack back in his pocket. He heaved a long, shuddery breath. "I feel like I can't, but I have to," he said. "He's my brother."

We walked up to the table. David didn't say a thing. Big tears like raindrops splashed on his hands and one fell on Gabriel's cheek.

"Dad's not done with him yet," I said, to say something, to try to make him feel better. Luckily he didn't hear me.

David didn't stay long. He came back into the office, rubbing his eyes with his sleeve. He said he didn't know how they wanted the service, that things were still up in the air.

"My mother—," he began, then left it there.

"No problem," I said. "Take all the time you need." I told him we'd be in touch.

My father and Clyde Bridges came into the office shortly after David left.

"My God, what stinks?" My father opened a window.

"David McCloud was just here. He said—"

"No sense talking to him. He's a drunk."

My father sat down and offered Clyde a cigar from the silver box on his desk. Clyde's in real estate. When an old person dies, Clyde's usually the one who puts the house on the market. He hears about it first. He and my father are friends.

"I'm going out for a while," I said. "I want to help look for Jennie."

My father waved the words away. "There's no sense in the whole town getting hysterical, just because some teen-ager wants attention."

"You know how this town is," Clyde said, chuckling.

I said, "Mrs. Harding called. They're afraid Jennie might kill herself, because she loved Gabe so much, and it turns out she's pregnant."

My father almost smiled. He said, "That figures."

"I told her I'd help."

"I need you here."

"Mom can answer the phone."

"You heard what I said. Clyde and I have business." He dismissed me.

I figured I knew what they needed to discuss. I lingered out of sight, to listen. The Sea Horse Festival, a brainchild of Clyde's, is scheduled to be held this weekend.

"People are saying we should postpone it," I heard Clyde say, "because Gabe's dead and everybody's sad."

"People die every day."

"Lucky for you." Clyde laughed.

Mendocino gets most of the tourists to the coast. Willow Creek is a few miles inland. Clyde came up with the Sea Horse Festival as a promotion, combining our location near the coast with what he calls "the pioneer spirit bit." He's hoping it will catch on and become an annual event. Then people will buy gas at Clyde's gas station and eat meals in Clyde's restaurant and spend the night in Clyde's motel, and we'll all be so grateful, we'll change the town's name to Clydesdale—

"Why couldn't Gabe have gotten killed next week?" he said. "We all knew this was going to happen. The only question was when. Count on the McClouds to screw things up."

My father said, "Gabe had a lot of friends."

"Sure, I liked Gabe. He was a nice enough kid. Could've been one hell of a quarterback if he hadn't got kicked off the team. Your kid ever play?"

"No," my father said.

"Well, the show must go on. We can't cancel it now. I'd still have to pay the band and the clown. Everybody's sad, but a week from now it will be back to business as usual," Clyde said. "Some kid gets killed, everybody's all worked up. They blame it on society. They blame it on the family. The kid's friends swear they won't drink anymore. The next weekend, they're having a big beer party at the cemetery, knocking over tombstones. You know what I'm saying."

I could picture my father's nod. He said, "I see it all the time."

"What a pickle." Clyde sighed. "What a can of worms. If I don't have the festival, I'm out a bundle, and if I do have it, everyone will hate me. I try to put this town on the map and people just think I'm being greedy. There's nothing wrong with making a profit. That's how you stay in business."

"It's up to you," my father said. "It's your baby."

"It's not like it'd bother Gabe," Clyde said. "He'd probably want people to have some fun. Maybe we could dedicate the whole thing to his memory."

I was on my way out, but before I left I had to make a few phone calls.

25

Carolyn Sanders

I just got off the phone with Jennie's mother. She was practically hysterical. She's convinced that Jennie's going to kill herself because she's pregnant.

I said, "I'm sure she wouldn't do a thing like that. She's probably just upset."

That's why they pay me the big money, folks: for brilliant observations like that. Of course she's upset. She's devastated. She really believed that she and Gabe would stay together; that love would conquer all their problems.

Mrs. Harding talks as if Jennie has died. In a sense, she has; the little girl is gone. A woman has been sleeping in Jennie's bed, masquerading as the dutiful daughter. How odd it must be to have a baby, who changes into a toddler, who becomes a child, who becomes an adult. . . . Do mothers mourn those lost babies, unreachable as the unborn?

I have no children. I have many children: all the students who pass through my classes, a steady stream of

85

eager faces, untapped potential, bored yawns. They can't wait to grow up and become adults, because they think we're always free to do what we want.

Surprise, surprise.

I had spoken to Mrs. Harding on the phone in the main office. She had begun to cry.

I said, "Sharon, please don't worry. May I call you Sharon?"

"Yes, that's fine."

"I'm sure Jennie's going to be all right."

"We can't find her!" she sobbed.

"Gabe's death must be a terrible shock for her. She probably just wants to be alone for a while."

"She's pregnant!" Mrs. Harding almost screamed, as if I must be stupid or deaf. "How could she do this? She's ruined her life!"

It's too bad she's pregnant, but I'm not surprised. Kids think they are immune from disaster; that "just this once" it will be okay if they make love, don't wear a seat belt, drink and drive.

"She hasn't ruined her life." I had to raise my voice over the argument escalating behind me. The kids and some of the teachers wanted to lower the flag to half-mast. The principal, flanked by his pet pit bull, Coach Decker, turned them down.

"This is not the end of the world," I told Sharon. I could feel myself getting angry. "It's too bad she's pregnant, but it's not a tragedy. Gabe's death is a tragedy. His life is over. He'll never get another chance. Your daughter is alive."

"She was going to go to college!"

"She can still go to college!"

"Not with a baby! She's too young to be a mother! She's going to have to put it up for adoption."

"You'll have plenty of time to discuss that," I said. "Your daughter will be home for dinner tonight. She'll sleep in her own bed. Gabriel's dead! He's never coming home! Do you understand what I'm saying? Imagine how his parents must feel. Not that they ever gave a damn when it could've done some good. They crippled that kid! That beautiful child!"

"Mrs. Sanders!" The principal, Dick Peterson, was standing in front of me. Everyone was watching us. He said, "That's quite enough. I need to talk to you. Please come into my office."

I told Sharon I would call her back. Then I told Dick, "We have nothing to discuss."

He flushed, appalled to have an audience. "You seem to be losing your grip," he said.

"I'm losing my grip because I'm so upset? Gabe's dead! How am I supposed to react?" I turned to Decker. "As for you, you little twerp, you're just another backyard fascist. You didn't like Gabe because he wouldn't salute. Now you're saying we can't have the flag at half-mast because it might give the kids the idea that he mattered. Let me tell you something, Decker—"

"Mrs. Sanders," Dick pleaded.

"—Gabe mattered. He mattered a lot! You're jealous of Gabe, the good-for-nothing bum. That's what you used to call him, remember? I'll tell you something, Decker: You'll have to raffle off door prizes to get people to come to your funeral!"

I left the office. It was break time. Kids were swarming in the halls. A few of them were waiting outside my room. They wanted to talk to me.

We went inside. I wanted to lock the door, to keep them with me, to keep them safe. The world is such a dangerous place. It gets crazier every day. We expect these kids to cope with so much. We fill the kiddy pool with sharks, then toss the children in. Have fun, we say, but don't get killed. Then we wonder why they numb themselves with drugs.

The kids crowded close to me, their faces stained with tears. They wanted to do something special for Gabe's funeral; to fill the place with flowers and his favorite music, all the stuff that he would really like.

This is the room where I begged him not to quit school. He was so close to graduating. He leaned against the blackboard with a smile on his face.

"Gabe, why are you doing this?" I said.

"No reason." He shrugged. "I'm just bored."

"You think you'll have more fun at the mill?"

"At least I'll get paid."

"That's peanuts. That's nothing." I wanted to shake him. "You can't make any real money without an education."

"There's more to life than making money," he said. "That's what you always tell us."

He'd do that: twist whatever you were saying so it bent around and bit you. I was angry.

I said, "Why are you pretending to be so stupid?"

He stopped smiling. "Why are you pretending to be so smart?"

One girl stayed behind when the other kids left. "Mrs. Sanders, can I ask you something?" she said.

"Certainly, Amy."

"Does it hurt to die?" She ran her fingers through her hair until her bangs stood up straight. "I mean, when Gabe died, do you think he felt it?"

"I don't know," I said. "It happened so fast. Maybe for just a second."

"Does it hurt most people?"

"Are you worried about that, Amy?"

She nodded, too distraught to speak.

"I imagine it's different for everyone," I said. "I doubt that the moment of death is too painful. Your heart just stops beating."

Tears were running down her cheeks. "But it seems

like it would hurt," she said. "And nobody would be there with me."

"When you die, you mean? Or after you're dead?"

"Both. The last, mostly. What happens to you then? I mean, after you die, where do you go?"

"It depends on what your beliefs are, Amy," I said. "Some people believe in heaven. Some don't. Some people believe in reincarnation: that you're born again as someone or something else."

"What do you believe?"

I took a deep breath. I'm supposed to guide these kids, not lead them. "I believe different things at different times," I said.

"Do you think Gabe's in heaven?"

"If heaven exists, I'm sure Gabe would be welcome. And some part of him will always be alive in our memories."

"That's what I think," she said. "I'm going to the funeral. Everybody's going, 'cause they love him so much. I'm scared when I die nobody will come to my funeral. Just my parents and brother. Nobody else would care."

"Amy, that's not true. Lots of people would care. Because the thing is, honey, we're all connected; every one of us on this planet. When we're mean to people, they pass along meanness. When we love them, they pass along love." My eyes filled up. She noticed and looked frightened. I blinked away the tears. I'm supposed to be an adult. "That's why it's so important to be kind and helpful whenever we can; to treat others the way we want to be treated. Do you understand what I'm saying?"

"I guess so." She looked doubtful. "But I still don't want to die."

I had to smile. "That makes two of us."

26

Gabriel McCloud

Dear Mrs. Sanders,

Thanks for coming hear Jennie play the other night. The band sounded great. The thing I like about her flute playing is she sounds like she does when she's talking know what I mean? If I played an instrument it would be the drum KABOOM my dad wouldn't go for that. Another thing I wanted to play was the piano but anyway its to late for that but it sure makes me proud to hear Jennie! I want our kids to play some instruments. If we have some I mean.

David was glad you said to say hi to him. He's standing here now and he says be sure to say hi back.

HI BACK! Now he's punching my arm.

Jennie sure looked pretty the other night. She looked like an angle in that dress. Sometimes I don't know what she's doing with me (I bet you wonder that to a lot of people do.) Its my hidden charm. On the outside all you see is a stupid old redneck like all these boys in town but inside where it really counts I'm smooth and smart and full of power. Like Shadow Man that's me! One thing about this town you get in a rut. Like your a jock or a brain or a doper or a redneck and people allways see you that way because they knew you since you were a kid. Maybe you've changed and your different then they think but they don't know that.

I keep meaning to bring in a Shadow Man for you to see but you'd probly think it was stupid. But I'm telling you the drawing is really good and the words are like poems. I like the way he talks people really stop and lissen. The other day Shadow Man was helping this little boy who didn't have any family and you could see it made the boy feel good like he finally had a big brother. It made Shadow Man feel good to he's alone a lot. He had a girlfriend for a while but it didn't work out but he still loves her. Some of the fans don't go for that stuff they write in letters in the back of each issue. They want Shadow Man to be like all the other super heros there allways fighting nazis and monsters. Who cares about that crap pardon my french. Why do people say that? Its not really french. In french its crapola.

I don't have much to say (as you can tell) I just want to say thanks for coming to the concert. Its nice to see a friendly face. Jennie's folks allways look like they could kill me I guess you can't blame them they probly wish I'd go away but this boy is here to stay.

What the hell do you do with these little things ' ' ' '??
Here's a few more I have some left over ' ' ' ' ' ' ' ' ' ' ' ' '

Gabriel:
You're right, the concert was wonderful. Hearing that beautiful music brings tears to my eyes.
I'd love to see a copy of **Shadow Man.** *I'll probably even want to borrow it!*
As for the apostrophes ('): You don't quite seem to have the hang of that yet. Drop by my room during lunch or after class someday, and we'll work on it.

C.S.

27

Jennie Harding

The tide has begun to come back in. The shift is too subtle to see. I feel it turning with my skin, as if someone is watching me.

If I don't leave the rock soon, the rock will be gone. The baby will be gone and so will I. The sun has melted my mind; I'm paralyzed. I'm stuck here like this rock, trying not to feel anything.

My mother always says she wants us to be close, but she's afraid to hear what I think. Her eyelids flicker when we discuss certain things, as if she's pulling down the shades. No one's home. Imagine how she'll look when she finds out I'm pregnant; as if she'd just heard that I'd died. My daughter is dead; I don't know this slut. . . . They've never thought Gabriel was good enough for me.

We argued about him endlessly. My mother would cry and my father would rage. You're ruining your life! he'd shout. As if his fragile baby could be smashed like a vase.

They only saw Gabe's hide, rough as abalone shell. He showed me the other side, the mother-of-pearl. He brought me bouquets of wildflowers. You are so pretty and smart! he'd say. I'm so proud of you, honey girl.

Recently, after a fight with his dad, Gabe said we should run away. I told him I couldn't do that to my family. He said he was my family. He was angry.

He said we should start a brand-new life, just him and me and the baby. Forget about the past; it doesn't matter, he said. But the past was wrapped around him like seaweed. He was drowning in the past. He couldn't see that.

I'd say, Can't you admit your family's screwed up? Why won't you see a counselor?

Talk to some stranger? he'd say, sneering. That don't do any good. Anyway, your parents aren't that great.

He thought that facing the truth about his family was the same thing as betraying them.

They've never told each other, I love you. Not once in their whole lives. He was starved for love. But the hunger made him mean. He would wound me with words that were hard to forget. I could tell when he'd been with another girl: her smell still on him, tiny bruises on his throat. I never understood if he wanted me to know or if he thought I was too dumb to notice.

That was why I wanted to break up with Gabe. I didn't want to be part of some game that he didn't even know he was playing. I didn't want to be hurt, or catch some kind of disease.

Instead, I got pregnant.

Won't people be shocked? She was such a good girl.

Who would've thought? She's come down in the world. Little Miss Honor Roll, look at her now, with her belly full of Gabe McCloud's baby.

The world is such an awful place. I don't want this child to suffer, to ever feel sadness or despair or pain. Babies die every day. They're killed, they starve. The old cemetery is full of little children, wiped out by ancient epidemics. We were up there one night. Some of the kids were getting rowdy, tipping over gravestones. Gabe made them stop. He replaced a stone that had toppled over. The inscription on it read:

'TIS A LITTLE GRAVE, BUT, OH, HAVE CARE,
FOR WORLDWIDE HOPES ARE BURIED THERE.
HOW MUCH OF LIGHT, HOW MUCH OF JOY,
IS BURIED WITH THIS DARLING BOY.

He was three years old. He died in 1887. I cried as if I'd lost him myself.

The waves lap gently at this rock. In time they will erase it. A hundred years from now all the people in our town will be gone, replaced by a fresh crop of faces. Even my baby would be a memory, or a very old man or woman.

Life is so sad. I cannot stand it. You're born, you live for a while, you die. Gabe just took a shortcut.

Oh, Gabe, I could kill you! Why did you leave me? I loved you so much, but it was never enough. You promised you'd change! You said you wanted this baby!

I'm too stupid to live. I am such a fool.

Gabe's dog is on the beach. I can't believe it. He's trotting across the sand. Jack sees me and wags his tail, then picks his way along the slick stone steps until he is beside me, his head in my hands. The waves are sliding over the stones. Soon they will erase his path.

28

Gerald McCloud

When I saw James's Harley it was like, it was like—the thing I'd been looking for all my life. Like mountains of money, or the best sex ever, when you shoot straight ahead and your brain explodes.

I saw that shiny bike and I thought: James's toy. And the pain in my brain went away that sudden, and the music on the radio was exactly right; the Stones were screaming and my body was electric and I knew in my heart: I'm not dead, I'm alive. Gabe may be dead, but I'm not going with him. I'm here, right now, and full of power, and I had to smile, I felt so high.

The Harley was parked in front of the liquor store. James had to be in there, getting his fix. I slowed way down and all the music stopped. There was a clock inside me and it was ticking, ticking.

I turned the truck real slow, oh so deliberate, and hit that Harley and drove it up on the sidewalk, into the beauty parlor wall. I could feel it crumpling, it was all slow motion, and I could see the faces of the women inside; their hair pinned flat or fat with rollers, scared, you know, jumping out of their chairs.

I heard metal crunching. I felt my left front fender cracking like an egg, but I didn't care. That shiny little toy was scrunched down to nothing. Maybe I was hurting, but James was destroyed.

Everyone comes running. You should see their faces. Mouths wide open, their eyes so shocked. I can't help laughing. I get out of my truck. Now James comes running from the liquor store, his face crumpled up like his little toy bike. Then we hunch and hug and punch each other, and for the first time today I know I'm going to be all right. It doesn't matter what's happened, it doesn't matter, Ma hurting, it doesn't matter my father keeps kicking me in the butt, kicking me, kicking me, trying to make me cry. You can kick me till I die, but I'll spit in your eye. You're not going to break me. You can go to hell.

There are people all around us, but they don't try to stop us. James's face is one big eye. I close it.

29

Sheriff Kevin Reese

Soon as I heard the news about Gabe, I figured that something like this would happen. I've got Gerald locked up. James is going to be okay. His nose is broken, but he did some damage too; Gerald's face looks like a pound of beef.

I was just back there, trying to talk to him, but it's like talking to a dog. A mean one.

He was stretched out on the bunk with his face to the wall. "I've got nothing to say to you," he said.

"You sure as hell do. Hasn't your mother got enough trouble, without you doing some stupid thing like this?"

"Get ahold of my father. He'll bail me out."

"You're going to the county jail," I said, "soon as I can arrange transportation."

He was on his feet, his hands on the bars. "What for?"

"Assault with a deadly weapon."

"He wasn't even on the damn bike!"

"I'm just telling you how it is," I said. "There's rules, you know, Gerald, and you broke them."

"What about that bastard? He killed my brother!"

"Quit blaming everybody else. I'm going to tell you something, Gerald: You better get yourself together. This is pretty serious business."

I gave him a smoke. He was all hunched over. He must've been hurting, but he wouldn't admit it. The funny thing is, I felt sorry for the kid. I've watched him grow up, through those bars.

I could've told you how that family was going to turn out. It was like a book you didn't need to read to know the end. I must've stopped Frank and David for driving drunk a hundred times. I'd say: You want to kill yourselves? Fine, do it at home. Don't go involving a bunch of innocent people.

David's never been the brightest part of the day, but he'd hate like hell to hurt anybody. He doesn't have a license now and Frank quit drinking. Or had until today. I expect later on I'll get a call from some bar, saying he's drunk and tearing the place apart.

He loved that boy. We all did. Gabe was a funny kid. Funny, as in he could make you laugh, and funny odd too, the moods he'd get in. That reminded me of his father. One second they'd be laughing and smiling; the next second their eyes would be blank.

Seemed like I pulled Gabe over every other day. That truck he drove was ancient, the same age as Frank's, and it was always missing a taillight or something.

Last week I flagged him down just outside town. When

I walked up to the window, he said, "Howdy, Sheriff!" like I was just the guy he'd been wanting to see.

I said, "Gabe, I noticed your turn signal's out, the right one. Unless you just forgot to signal."

"I'd never forget a thing like that," he said. "It must be the bulb. I'll fix it."

"Man," I said, taking a good look at the truck, "this thing has seen better days."

"Yeah, about thirty years ago," he said. "I'm restoring it to its original condition: a hunk of metal."

I laughed. I said, "I also noticed your brake light's out. How's the emergency brake?"

"Just fine. Take a look for yourself." He pulled the brake handle out and handed it to me.

He was a good kid. No matter what he did, you couldn't stay mad at him.

I asked Gerald if he wanted me to call his uncle Tom, who could maybe get him a lawyer. He was going to need one.

"No." He looked disgusted. "He wouldn't help me."

"Your father's not home now. What about David?"

Gerald snorted. "He can't even dial the phone."

"Then you'll have to sit tight till I find your dad."

"Check the bars," Gerald said, sneering.

I went back into my office and called up Tom. He said he wouldn't come down to talk to Gerald.

"Leave him there," Tom said. "That's where he belongs."

"His mother's got one boy at the funeral home. She doesn't need another one in jail."

"Gerald should've thought of that!"

"Gerald doesn't think," I said. "How's Katherine doing? I hear she's in shock."

"I don't know how she's doing! I haven't been out there."

"There's no need to yell, Tom. I just wanted you to know that I've got Gerald."

"Well, keep him." He hung up.

Gerald must've heard my side of the conversation. He laughed and said, "I told you he couldn't care less! Who needs him?"

30

James Wilkins

I'm going to get me a lawyer and sue that bastard for everything he's got. Busted up my bike, squashed it like a bug, standing there laughing like it's some big joke. Gerald thinks he can act as crazy as he wants and get away with it.

No go, Joe. The party's over.

My damn nose is killing me. My brother said, "If you feel like you look, you're hurting."

He says I should get a lawyer and sue for the bike and all my pain and suffering.

Gabe's the one who should sue for pain and suffering! He had to live in that family. Crazy as loons, the whole damn bunch of them, and he was crazy for staying. He should've run away. Anything was better than what they done to him.

One time he came over here, years ago, maybe we were nine or ten. His nose was bloody and his eye was puffed up. He didn't say nothing; he just stood on the porch.

I said, "Your old man whipped you, didn't he?"

"No," Gabe said. "I fell off my bike."

"That's not true. Your old man hit you."

"No," Gabe said. He kept saying no. But he didn't say Gerald or David did it. So I knew it was his father, and it made me mad that he'd bullshit me like that.

"You're a liar," I said. So we got in a fight, and all the time we hit each other, I kept saying, "Liar, he whipped you," and Gabe kept saying no.

Then my mother came out and broke it up, and Gabe came in and had dinner. He ate at our house a lot when he was little. My mom never liked to send him home. She thought the way they treated him was wrong, but there wasn't nothing she could do. He was their kid, they could treat him any way they wanted.

Gabe's never going to show up at the door again. He's never going to tell me I'm so ugly it's pathetic. We're never going diving or hunting or fishing.

It took a long time, but they finally killed him.

31

Donald Morrison

I used the phone in the upstairs hallway. The door to my mother's den was closed. I could hear her laughing. She watches a channel that features reruns of old comedy shows. Supposedly she's in there doing the ironing. She hardly ever leaves that room, or the past.

The first number I dialed was in Mendocino. A man's voice answered.

"Hello," I said. "I'm calling for Skedaddle the clown."

"This is Skedaddle," the man said.

I pictured him wearing a big wig and red nose, but he probably doesn't hang around the house like that.

"This is Donald Morrison, from the Morrison Funeral Home."

"My God!" he gasped. "What's wrong? What's happened?"

"Nothing's wrong," I assured him. "I just wanted you to know that the Sea Horse Festival will be postponed. One of Willow Creek's finest young men has died, and it wouldn't be right to hold a celebration now. Mr. Clyde Bridges asked me to inform you."

I felt like a tiny boat way out on the ocean. Each word I spoke pushed me farther from shore. Maybe my father was right, and I was weak and soft. Or maybe he was wrong and I was finally on my own.

"He told me he'd pay me, rain or shine," Skedaddle said.

"Mr. Bridges's word is as good as gold. And of course he'll want you there when the festival is rescheduled."

"Tell him he's got to let me know in advance."

"I imagine you're a pretty busy clown," I said.

The top of my head felt tight and tingly. A smile kept twitching at the corners of my mouth. If I'd looked in a mirror then, I would have seen a stranger, or maybe Gabe's eyes, peeking out of my own.

I called the singer in the band that was supposed to play, a country-western group called Patty and the Posse. Patty was amazed that Clyde was canceling the event.

"Who would've thought?" she said. "He hardly seems human."

"People are full of surprises," I said.

I arranged for a sign to be painted and displayed downtown. It would read: IN LOVING MEMORY OF GABRIEL MCCLOUD, THE SEA HORSE FESTIVAL WILL NOT BE HELD TODAY.

I called up and informed Mrs. Louise Gates, whose church group ladies were catering the food for the event.

"Oh, Donald, it's no problem. We can freeze the cheese puffs," she said. "Or maybe we could give all the food to his family, for the gathering after the funeral. They're having a funeral, aren't they?"

"I'm sure they will," I said. "Some of the details aren't settled yet. The family is pretty upset."

"Of course they are." She sighed. "It's such a terrible thing. A nice boy like Gabe. Mind you, he was no angel, but who could be, with a father like that? Donald, I don't mean to pry, but I heard that, well, that Gabe had been . . . dismembered."

"From his family, you mean?" I couldn't help myself. It always surprises me how even the nicest people can't get enough blood in their diets.

"I mean," she said delicately, "how should I put this— I heard that Gabe had been decapitated. That his head came off."

"Oh, that's not true," I said. "As a matter of fact, we can't find the entire body. We think he went straight to heaven."

There was a thoughtful pause. She couldn't disagree, believing, as she does, that such things are possible.

"It's a difficult situation," I said. "Please keep it under your hat. I'll be in touch about the food."

"Of course," Louise said. "I think it's wonderful of Clyde to respond like this. Who would've expected it? He's already paid for the groceries and everything."

"It's funny, but sometimes death brings out the best in

people," I said. "Wait, here's my father. He says they found Gabe. I'd better go now. Good-bye, Mrs. Gates."

My mother was watching "I Love Lucy." She laughed at something Ethel said to Fred. I wrote a check to Clyde, from my personal account, covering all his expenses. I left this on the front seat of his car. Then I headed toward the Hardings' house.

32

Gabriel McCloud

I am so sick of writing in this book. It seems like a waste of time. I'm not going to college. That's all Jennie talks about. She still has another year of high school. She could get a good job right here in town. She won't need to work I'll be making good money. That's the trouble with women they run you around. My mother's not like that she never had a job but latly she says she wish she did probly so she could leave us. I am sick of them fighting all the time. My father says something then she says something then David gets in the act because he hates it when they fight I think he has an ulcer or something his stomack hurts. I feel like yelling EVERYBODY SHUT UP but instead I leave the house and drive around or go see Jennie. She calms me down exsept when she talks about leaving town. I'm not scared to leave I like it here. She thinks she's to good for Willow Creek.

I feel bad today I guess you can tell. The new issue of Shadow Man came its going to be the last one it says in the back. They say it didn't catch on the readers wanted more action. They didn't even let him go back to his planet or put him in with the other super heros those guys are a bunch of jerks. They just killed him.

I can't believe they'd do that but they did. I keep looking and looking at it. Shadow Man gos to the Creator of Creation who gave all the super heros thier powers (not his parents they were only taking care of him) and the Creator sees how sad he is and says Shadow Man what's the matter? Shadow Man says (I'm copying it down so you can see the words I wish you could see the pictures) "I am cold, Creator, and I cannot get warm. I am hungry and I cannot eat. I am surrounded by crowds yet I am always alone. I am exhausted and I cannot sleep." The Creator says "Ask for what you want, my son, and it is yours." The Creator loves Shadow Man like his own son. And Shadow Man says "Let the fighting cease, all around the world, in every land." The Creator looks real sad and says "With all my power, I cannot do that." So Shadow Man says "Then give ME peace. Blind my eyes to sorrow. Fill my ears with silence. All I hear is weeping and screams. The world is a terrible place, Creator." The Creator says "Sleep, my child; the world is only a dream."

WHEN SHADOW MAN DIED THE HEAVENS WEPT WHILE THE EARTH SLEPT BELOW IN IGNORANCE.

That's how it ends and if you want my opinyin it sucks

big time. Anyway its only a stupid comic I'm just really in a bad mood today sorry about that.

G. Mc.

Gabriel:
Why don't you write to the editors and tell them your opinion? Publishers want to please their readers. If they hear from enough people, they'll bring Shadow Man *back. The address is on the fan page or in the front of the magazine. Give it a try. Don't give up on Shadow Man yet!*

C.S.

33

Tom Dawson

I've spent all morning on the phone, calling our relatives around the country; my sisters and their families.

They all want to know how Katherine's doing. I say I haven't talked to her yet. Then there's a long pause and sometimes there's an argument. A couple of my sisters are on their way. They say no one answers Katherine's phone.

Even Becky says I should go over there. A while ago she came down to the store. She looked so small and out of place here. Usually I just see her at home.

"You have to go see your sister," she said. "I know how you feel and why you feel that way, but none of that matters now. Gabriel's dead."

"Don't you think I know that? Who do you think pried him out of that truck? Whose blood was all over my clothes?"

"Listen to me, mister: I washed those clothes. You're not the only one who's suffering. I loved him too." She brushed away tears.

I noticed that Bud Carter was eyeing us while pretending to examine a saw.

"Bud, do you mind if we have some privacy here?" I said. "We're talking about our family."

He left in a huff. He would've charged the saw anyway. Becky put her hand on my shoulder.

She said, "That's the point I'm trying to make, hon. We're talking about our family. Those are your people, whether you like it or not."

"They're all screwed up."

"Who's not?" she said. "Anyway, nobody's asking for your opinion. They need you, Tom. You owe it to your sister."

I used to try to help Katherine. She wouldn't listen. She wouldn't leave him, no matter what. No matter how many other women he was seeing. No matter how bad he was to the children. She stayed in that marriage like it was revenge. I told her: You don't have to teach him a lesson. Leave him to life. It'll get him. It gets everyone.

If my mother were alive, there would be no question: I would go to Katherine's house. She held the family together. Now that she's dead, do her wishes still count? I love my mother. Does she still love me?

My heart is so heavy it hurts to breathe. There's nothing worse than the death of a child. When they go, they take the future with them. And Gabe was a baby, even though he was big. All through his childhood I tried to help him, but Franny was still his father. He didn't seem to want his boys to get ahead. Like if they got too tall, they'd look down on him.

One time, when things were really bad, I told Gabe: "This isn't going to last forever. Someday you'll be on your own and you can live your life any way you want."

I didn't understand then, like I do now, that you never leave the past behind. It haunts you.

Mama lost a child. Harry died in his sleep. He was just a baby, born between Judy and me. Sometimes Mama cried when she talked about him, even though he'd been dead for almost half a century. When we were all grown up she did her laundry with that baby soap because it brought back happy memories. Becky does the same thing with that baby lotion. She claims it's the only thing that softens her hands.

I keep thinking what I'd say to Katherine, if I saw her. I'd tell her how sorry I am about Gabe, about everything. I'd tell her I wish I could take some of her pain, so she wouldn't have so much to endure. Hold my hand, I'd say; I won't let go. When the darkness pulls you under, I'll be there too.

I'd tell her what I know from losing Kay. There isn't a day that I don't think about her. Not that I don't love Becky and our boys. But Kay was my first wife, my woman, my world. When she died, I would've died, if I'd had the choice. But I didn't; the twins were depending on me.

A lot of years have gone by and the loss is still there. It's like a hole in your heart, but it doesn't kill you. It doesn't get better; it just gets different. You learn to live with it.

34

Carolyn Sanders

Maybe I don't know what's important anymore. Maybe I'm overreacting.

So Gabriel is dead. Let's not lose our heads.

But if love's not the point, what's the answer?

I'm outside, on the school's front lawn, lowering the flag to half-mast. The rope runs through my fingers, inch by inch. I can feel the staring faces at the windows. They think I'm crazy. Which is terribly convenient: They leave me alone.

That little piece of cloth flaps in the breeze; the red, white, and blue, flying over our dreams. I've never lowered, or raised, a flag before, but when I got out here, I knew just what to do, as if the knowledge was in my blood, my fingertips. It's my flag too, not just Decker's.

It's lowered to half-mast when a head of state dies. Someone really important, like the president. What is more important than the life of a child? We lose a thousand Gabriels every day.

Oh, let's all drive as fast as we can, smash into one

another and drive off cliffs; quench our thirst for revenge with blood, and taste our enemy's death on our lips; destroy our pain and kill our suffering, so that life will never hurt us again. Amen.

Gabe, I didn't want it to turn out like this. I could see this coming down the road for years. I couldn't stop it; I could only watch it. We all let you down, not only your parents, who loved you as much as they knew how, but it wasn't enough. It was never enough.

We'll miss you, honey. Forgive us.

35

Jennie Harding

I've tried to make Jack leave the rock. The waves are rolling in. Soon they'll cut us off from shore and then they'll devour the throne.

"Get out of here, you stupid dog!" I point toward the beach and stamp my feet. He looks at me, his eyes reproachful.

"Get out of here, you stupid mutt!" Gabe yelled the other night, when he was drunk. "Beat it! I don't want you around!" He kicked the dog, but Jack crouched down, as if saying: I won't run away; do what you will, I'll still love you.

I would never have gotten in the truck that night if I'd realized he'd been drinking. By the time I knew that it was more than a bad mood, we were parked in the middle of nowhere.

"Look at you," I'd said. "You're acting just like your father. Why do you have to be so mean?"

"Shut up," he snarled. "I'm sick of listening to you."

"And I'm sick of you acting like this," I said. "I won't let you drink around the baby."

"That suits me fine. Maybe it's not even mine."

I felt as if he'd kicked me in the stomach. In the dim light inside the truck his face looked like a stranger's.

"Gabriel, how can you say a thing like that?"

"I'm sick of you ragging on me all the time! This is the real me! Take it or leave it!"

"And I'm sick of watching you kill yourself with booze! If you hate life so much, why don't you just blow your head off?"

"Maybe I will!" he roared. He kicked me out of the truck; actually kicked and pushed me out. Then he went around back and dragged Jack out, leaving us there, by the side of the road. We waited in the dark for Gabe to come back for us, then we walked home. That was two nights ago. It was the last time that Gabe and I spoke.

Usually, after we fought, he'd call and apologize. I'm sorry, honey girl; it won't happen again. He'd say he was going to quit drinking so much. He'd promise that things were going to change.

This time he didn't call me and I didn't call him. I was too angry. I was too proud. This is the last straw, I thought; I've had it.

We were supposed to go to Mendocino for dinner this weekend. Gabe told me about it on Monday night, the night before he turned on me. We were parked in his truck, in front of my house. Gabe had his hand on my belly. My folks were inside, watching the news on TV. I thought: Wait till they hear the news about this baby.

He told me he'd made a reservation at Collins House, a beautiful old inn overlooking the sea. I said he shouldn't do that; it's too expensive. He doesn't make much money at the planter box factory.

"We're going," he said. "You deserve the best. We'll have a nice dinner Saturday night, just you and me and Jasper." That's what he jokingly calls the baby. He's sure it's going to be a boy. Gabe patted my belly. "It's hard to believe he's really in there. How does he breathe?"

"Through the cord, I think. It's complicated. Gabe, we've got to plan this out. We've got to tell our families."

"You're the one who's been putting it off. Honey, I want you to marry me."

I said, "Maybe we shouldn't get married right away." I'd always thought we would, someday, but things were happening too fast. I had to finish high school. And what about college? I was going to go to college. How could I be a wife and mother? I wasn't done with being a girl. I felt as if someone had handed me a script and said, Here, you play the woman.

"Why not?" Gabe said. "That's what people usually do, especially when they're going to have a baby. Besides, I love you."

"I love you too. But that doesn't mean we need to get married."

Gabe looked mad. He said, "Most girls in town, they'd jump at the chance, if I asked them."

"Then go ahead and ask them! How about Susie Richards?"

"I hardly even know her."

"You must think I'm so stupid! I know what's been going on!"

"It ain't going on anymore," he said. "Anyway, she didn't mean nothing to me."

"Then why did you sleep with her?"

"What do you want me to do?" He hit the steering wheel, hard. "I'm not a little boy, I'm a man! You make love to me once, then cut me off! What difference does it make now? You're pregnant!"

"Thanks to you!"

"Hey, you were there too!"

He was right, of course. I'd written the script with my own hand.

He left abruptly, tires squealing. I went into the house. My mother sighed. My father gave me an elaborate frown.

Gabe called the next day. He'd said, "I'm sorry, honey. I'm sorry I've been acting so crazy. It's just that I've got a lot on my mind, with the baby and everything."

"It's the beer," I said. "You've got to stop."

"I wasn't drunk last night!"

"No, but you'd been drinking."

"Just a few brews. What's wrong with that?"

"You can't handle it," I said. "You're an alcoholic." That was the first time I'd let myself admit it.

"That's ridiculous," Gabe said. He joked about it; the problem wasn't him, it was all in my head. "You never want to have any fun," he said. "No wonder you want to be a teacher."

He came by after supper so we could go for a drive and talk. We were going to let Jack run on the beach. We never got that far. We started to argue. Gabe was scary. I'd never seen him so angry. I thought he was going to hit me.

He said an alcoholic was someone old like his father, or someone who drinks hard liquor, like David. Not someone like him, who enjoys a few beers. He said I was just making up excuses so I wouldn't have to marry him.

"That's not true!" I said. "Why won't you listen?"

" 'Cause you ain't the voice of God!"

He pushed me out of the truck. He'd never hurt me before. I could feel his hands on me long after he'd left. He looked like Gabe, but he'd become someone else. Someone I didn't know.

If you hate life so much, why don't you just blow your head off?

I play the scene in my mind, again and again, rewriting the lines for a happy ending. I should've held him tight and never let go. I should've said: You are a wonderful person. I should've told him: I'll always love you, but I won't live your mother's life. You're losing me. Time is running out. Save yourself: Gabe is dying.

I said all that, so many times. He never really heard

me. The other voices in his head were too loud: the screams and shouts, the little boys crying. The past always drowned me out.

I can't think anymore. I want to fall asleep and rest forever on the breast of the sea. The world could be so lovely if it weren't for people. We're cruel and greedy. We hurt each other. I hurt so bad. It has to stop. I'm sorry, little baby. Please forgive me, for bringing you here and then taking you away.

The air is thick with spray. Jack is pacing, worried.

"Get out of here, you idiot!" I point to the beach. "If you don't leave now, it will be too late!"

Too late. He looks sad. He leans his head against my leg. I bury my fingers in his thick coat and touch the leather collar Gabe made. The waves break in a white ring all around us.

36

Francis McCloud

I'm doing what I should've done a long time ago: I'm getting the hell out of this town. Everybody hates me. They'll be glad when I'm gone. They say, I'm sorry about Gabe. Or: How's Katherine taking it? Or they don't say nothing. They turn away. What do you say to a man who's lost his boy?

My boy is gone! I can't take it. It's like God's killed me, then woke me up so I can die again, every day. I could've sworn Tom saw me when I drove by the store, but he didn't even raise his hand. We're talking about his nephew! His sister's baby boy! And he looks right through me like we don't mean nothing! He hasn't even picked up the phone!

I'm going to drive down the highway till I get to San Diego, or maybe even Mexico. I've got to keep going, I've got to keep moving, 'cause if I don't keep moving, I'm drowning.

Why is he dead? He was such a good kid! He could've

been something. My son! He's not a bum like David or crazy like Gerald. There's something wrong with Gerald. You can see it in his eyes. If he was in a war, he wouldn't care which side, as long as he could kill somebody. The only person who can call him off is his mother and she won't say nothing. She's frozen hard. Damn you, Katherine! None of this would've happened if you'd loved me, but you didn't, you starved me. When we were young, you could eat me up, 'cause I was so sweet, that's what you said. Now it don't mean nothing, all those years together, the troubles we been through, the babies we made. I might as well be dead. I wish I was. I'd stop this truck and get down on my knees and say, God, take me and give back my son! Please, God! Please!

I'm going nuts. I'm screaming in this truck like someone can hear me. I have to have a drink. I am going to get drunk. No reason not to. No one to stop me. I could keep on driving, nobody would care, nobody would even try to find me.

Except for Jennie's father. He'd hunt me in hell. He looked like he wanted to kill me, downtown. Stopped his car right in the road and ran up to the truck.

"What the hell are you doing here?" he shouted. "You're supposed to be looking for Jennie!"

"I am," I said.

"In the liquor store?"

"I was getting some cigarettes, do you mind?"

"You listen to me!" His eyes were wild. "I know I should feel sorry for you, but I don't, God forgive me. I despise you. I want my daughter back!"

"You'll get her back," I said. "She'll turn up when she's ready."

"We can't take that chance! We've got to find her!"

"We could get more people to help us look."

"No," Harding said. "I don't want them to know she's pregnant."

"Are you kidding? They already know," I said. "This is a small town. What's more important: your daughter or your pride?"

"You talk about pride, you worthless bum? You killed your own son! You ruined his life!"

He was screaming at me. I got out of the truck. Joey Hammer ran up and grabbed me. He said, "Calm down, Franny. Just calm down. Wes is upset. He don't know what he's saying."

Ask Joey; he was there. It was an accident. The baby climbed out of his crib. He'd never done that before. He learned real quick. Then Katherine was screaming—

I've got to keep driving. I'm going to start over. This time I'm going to do things right. Some women think I'm still good-looking. Not my wife; she can't stand the sight of me. Thinks I'm a no-good drunk. I'll drink to that. Soon as I can find a place to pull over, I'm going to break open that bottle.

The ocean's so big it makes the sun seem small, like a

little toy ball. I should keep on driving. But then I'd never get to see my grandchild, Gabriel's son or daughter. Katherine had boys, so she might like a girl. I can picture the baby in my mind. She's got yellow hair and twinkly eyes. Her daddy looks so proud! He's laughing and tossing her into the air, and the baby's laughing too. Her mama's watching them, smiling.

But that's not Gabriel. Gabe is dead. That's not him and Jennie with the baby. The couple in the picture in my mind come close, and I'm looking at Katherine and me.

37

David McCloud

When Frank comes home, I'll have to tell him Gerald's in jail. Then he'll get mad like it's all my fault. Like, I'm the oldest, so I should set an example. As if anybody cares what I think. They think I'm a joke because I don't have any money, and if you don't have money, nobody takes you seriously.

I don't think that's right. You should get some points for doing your best. So maybe you aren't some big-time genius. Maybe you're just some guy on the bench. Maybe you don't even make the team. Maybe you're just some fan in the stands. Maybe you're the damn pigskin.

I shouldn't drink on an empty stomach. It gets me. Trouble is, once I start, I forget to eat. Sometimes Gabe would make me a sandwich. He'd say, Buck up, Sport! You gotta keep up your strength! It's a great life if you don't weaken.

I miss him so much. He's only been gone for half a day and sometimes I don't see him for weeks, like when I take off or get a job or something. But this time feels different.

His room looks so different. I was in there a while ago and nothing's changed; his clothes are everywhere, his bed's not made. But it just feels wrong, like a stranger's been in there. I laid down on the bed and put my head on his pillow. It smelled like Gabe.

Oh, Gabe. I'm dying.

While I was in there the phone started ringing, but it stopped by the time I got out here. I thought Ma might've got it, but her door was closed. The whole time I was with her she didn't say nothing, but at least she patted my head. That's something.

Then the phone rang again—it's been ringing all morning—and it was Sheriff Reese saying Gerald was down at the jail. So when Frank comes home, I'll have to give him the news. If he ever comes back again. It's like people keep leaving, but they don't come back. Like maybe this place is haunted. Like maybe if I opened my mother's door, the room would be empty. She'd be gone.

I wish Uncle Tom would call. He'd make things better. He used to be around a lot, before the big fight, when all that stuff got said. Everybody looked so sad and shocked. Then they got mad and started yelling.

I may not be too smart, but I'd sure do things different if I was king of the world. For instance, starting right now there'd be no hard feelings. People wouldn't say mean things, and if they did, they'd be sorry and apologize and people would forgive them.

There wouldn't be any yelling or hitting or wars or

killing. Everybody would be happy. And if you made a mistake, you could try again and nobody would laugh at you.

I should eat something. My hands are shaking. These cigarettes make me feel lousy. Pretty soon I'm going to get myself together; quit smoking and drinking, and start eating right, and take some vitamins, and get a job so Gabe would be proud of me. He always said, Don't let them get you down. Pick up the pieces one at a time and don't try to climb the mountain in an afternoon. Something like that. I knew what he meant. He always cheered me up.

I wish I could tell him, Thank you, Gabe. I wish I could say, I love you. I wish I could say, I'll always be your big brother and I will take care of you and none of this happened, and I'll give you a good example.

Oh, Gabe. Little buddy, little brother.

Someone's knocking on the door. I can't find my shirt, but I put on my sunglasses so people won't know I've been crying.

I open the door. Uncle Tom is on the porch. His face looks real old and tired. He hugs me and says, "I'm so sorry, David," and I'm bawling in his arms like a little boy.

38

Gabriel McCloud

Dear Mrs. Sanders,

I'm sorry what I said after class the other day. I didn't mean that stuff. Your a good teacher the best I ever had its not your falt I'm quitting school. But what's the use? I'll just end up at the mill so I might as well start now and make some fulltime money. Eight bucks an hour and medical benefits. I can use that my teeth are bugging me. I don't like the mill the saws are to loud they can really drive you crazy. They give us earplugs but they don't work good. The other thing I don't like is your hands get cold because there aren't any walls just these tin roofs and the wind freezes your fingers. But you might as well get use to it and then it won't bug you. Like Shadow Man! Ya! That guy could eat stones but it didn't do no good they pulled his plug.

Thanks for offering to help me write the people at the comic but it would just be a waste of time. They've already bumped him off or maybe he'll turn up fighting nazis or communists. I don't care that much its just a comic.

So anyway I just want to say I'm sorry I'm quitting and I won't graduate but I'll be there in spirit. Ya! With all my friends that's the one thing I'll miss. But there's no sense waiting to start my real life I might as well make some big time bucks. Maybe I'll even get you a present or pay for that book I lost. Ya!

Thanks a lot anyway. Yours Truely,

Gabe McCloud

39

Jennie Harding

This will kill my parents. They will think they failed me. I wish I could explain that it's not their fault. They were wonderful parents. They've always loved me.

But we don't live in a bubble. I've seen the world. I see it every night on the news on TV. We watch while we eat dinner. As I'm piling food on my plate, I'm looking at starving children. Or watching a story about something that's disappearing: elephants, the rain forests, the ozone layer. Or hearing about wars, lots of wars, or plane crashes or epidemics or serial killers.

Too much is wrong. It's too big; we can't fix it. I can't help anyone. I couldn't even save Gabe. As close as we were, I couldn't reach him.

The air is almost too wet to breathe. The waves are crashing. Jack is scared. I am stroking his fur, trying not to freak out. I'm afraid it will hurt when the water fills my lungs. I'm afraid I'll wish, too late, to change my mind.

I used to be scared about labor pains. Then I thought: It couldn't be too bad, or there wouldn't be so many babies.

My mother wanted lots of kids, but she had to have an operation. Once I asked her if it hurt to have me. A lot, she said, but you were worth it.

I wish I could tell my folks how much I love them, one more time, so they won't be sad. They would've been so mad when they found out about the baby. They would've said: How could you be so stupid?

I'm not ashamed of loving Gabe. Love takes strength; it's not a weakness. If you don't love people, you might as well be dead. Like Gabriel's father; he's a vampire, he drank up his whole family. I used to want to blow my top at him, but what was the point? He couldn't change the past. He couldn't even change himself.

I'm worried that Donald will take this badly. I'm one of his only friends. He's too shy to open up with most people. He's ashamed of his occupation.

One time I said, "If you don't like it, quit. There's no law that says you have to be a mortician."

He said, "My father would kill me."

"With a knife or a gun?"

"With a look," Donald said. But I'd made him smile and that's half the battle. "I mean, he acts like he's given me this wonderful gift and I'm too much of a knucklehead to appreciate it."

"If he wants to be a mortician, that's his business," I said. "But you don't have to carry on the family tradition. He only gets one life; he doesn't get yours."

"He gets everybody's, eventually," Donald said. His

mother has convinced him that she'll die if he leaves home, but she doesn't have to stay there; that's her choice. Donald should be free to do what he wants. He'd like to be a veterinarian. He'd be good at that, he's so kind and gentle. Donald is one of my favorite people.

I hope he doesn't take this personally. I hope he doesn't think: If she were really my friend, she would never have left me behind.

I didn't mean for this to happen. Killing myself was the furthest thing from my mind. I thought I'd be talking to Gabriel tonight, then this weekend we'd go to Mendocino—

The last wave hit the rock so hard the spray fell like hail. I'm so sorry Jack's here. I'm so sorry about the baby. She's depending on me and I'm betraying her. Gabe wanted a boy. I'm sure it's a girl. She stirs in her sleep. I pat my belly. Don't be scared, baby; Mommy's here.

I'm so sorry about my folks. I'm so sorry about everything. The last thing I ever wanted to do was hurt my family.

40

Francis McCloud

I park the truck and lean my head out the window. The sun feels good on my face, like warm hands. Me and Katherine would hold hands and watch the water and listen to the waves. They sound so peaceful. Like maybe it doesn't matter if you die, a thousand years from now the sea will still be breathing, the tide will still be going in and out.

I'm not surprised Gabe and Jennie had a special place. Kat and me had lots of special places; stretches of beach full of shells and bottle glass, or no undertow, so we could go skinny-dipping.

We always figured we made Timmy at this one place we had. We'd only been married for a couple of months. I wasn't too pleased when I found out. I'd wanted time together, just the two of us. Then she had him and he was so—beautiful. I couldn't believe we'd made him with our love. I'd stand there and watch him asleep in his crib and listen real close to make sure he was breathing. When Katherine nursed him I felt so proud, like this is my wife and my baby boy. I'll kill any man who hurts them.

And then that man was me.

After he died, it seemed like nothing was right. It wasn't the same between Katherine and me, even though we had the other babies. And I beat on the boys. I shouldn't have done that. That's what my father done to me and my brothers. We loved our mother, so we couldn't touch him, but after she died we cut him dead. We never went and saw him again. My brothers moved away to different parts of the country. I haven't seen them in years. Seems like loving our mama and hating our father was all we had in common.

I never meant to be like him with my boys. I wanted to kiss them and love them. But I couldn't; I was frozen, and that made me mad. It made me so mad I went crazy. There's no excuse, it's too late to change it. My wife and my sons hate me.

Once Kat told me, "You never loved me. You don't love me 'cause you don't know how."

I do the best I can, but nothing went the way I planned. It wasn't just Timmy; it was everything. Her brother calling me a crook, in my own house. Like I'm some low-life bum! The scum of the earth! All this crap about stuff that was none of his business. And what does Katherine do? She don't say nothing. She just looks at me!

Damn you, Gabe! Give me one good reason why I

shouldn't open this bottle and drink the whole damn thing. All you are is a ghost. You don't even exist. That ain't my boy at the funeral parlor. My boy is gone. He ran away. He'll be back someday. I almost killed him, drunk as a skunk on this same stuff. His mother looked scared, but he didn't. He said, "Go ahead and shoot me, you crazy old fart! You've already killed everybody in this house!"

Oh, Mama, please! It hurts so bad! God, do you hear me? If you hate me so much, why don't you kill me?

All I need is a sip, a taste to clear my head. I open the bottle and lift it to my lips—

My mouth fills with Gabriel's blood.

I'm choking and gagging. I spit it out. Everything I swallowed is coming back up. The bottle explodes against a rock.

If I was man enough, I'd blow my head off. Make everybody happy. They'd all be glad. But I'm too scared I'll go to hell, a special hell for men who kill their babies.

God, I'm sorry! God, please help me. I've thrown away the bottle. I've kept my vow. I've got to stay sober. I've got to find Jennie. I've got to help my wife, but I don't know how.

We used to lie on the beach and look up at the sky and plan how our life was going to be. I'd make lots of money and we'd buy a big house, and have a bunch of kids, and do some traveling.

The farthest I've ever been is Las Vegas. There was never enough money. We got bogged down. And by the time I figured out that the boys really loved me, they didn't even like me anymore.

Once when Gabe was little we went to the beach. We were on our way home from somewhere, him and me.

I took him to my and Katherine's favorite place, this pretty little cove where we made Timmy. It's hidden from the road. We had to climb down the path. It was real steep. Gabe was holding my hand.

We must've stayed down there for a couple of hours. I showed him how you could walk out across the water, to a rock that looked like a throne.

"We're the kings, Daddy!" Gabe loved that place. We had a picnic: a bag of potato chips and a bottle of Pepsi-Cola. Then we had to get off because the tide was coming in. We stood on shore and watched the throne disappear. Gabe started crying. "Don't worry," I said. "It's still there, you just can't see it."

All the way up the path, Gabe kept asking, "Can we come back, Daddy? When can we come back?"

"Soon," I said, but we never did. There was always too much going on.

Gabe didn't forget; he had a memory like an elephant. He'd say, Daddy, can we go back to that special place?

And then I realize that he'd found it on his own.

I start the truck and roar south down the highway. The turnout is just where I saw it in my mind, hidden behind blackberry bushes gone wild. There's a set of tire tracks in the sand. Another truck was here not long ago.

I run down the highway to the nick in the cliffs. The path's worn deep and feels familiar to my feet, like I'd walked it every night in my dreams.

When I get to the last turn, I look down on the beach. My heart starts pounding like the waves.

The rock has almost disappeared. It looks like Jennie and the dog are standing on the water.

41

Jennie Harding

The waves suck at my feet. Jack fell, but I grabbed him. He's soaked and shivering, pressed against my skirt. I'm fighting to keep my balance.

Why? If I wanted to die, I could let go right now and let the water claim me. What would it prove—that life is painful and pointless? More pointless than this?

How strange it would've been, on Tuesday night, if we could've looked ahead and seen all this coming. There were so many things I counted on, Gabe. This wasn't one of them.

I wanted to make the world a better place; to do something helpful, like be a good teacher. Ignorance breeds fear and fear breeds cruelty, and don't tell me that's not true, Gabe. Just take a good look at your father.

I wish I could see that man again. I'd say: Look what you've done. You destroyed your family. He wasn't alone. Gabe's mother helped him. Everybody talks like, Oh, poor Katherine, but she could've stopped him, she could've left.

I'd never stay with someone who hurt my children. You can't love somebody you fear.

And look at you, Gabe. You ran away from yourself until you couldn't run anymore, until you dropped with exhaustion. All you wanted was to be unconscious.

You must be in heaven now. Gabe, can you see me? What would you tell me, if you could?

The waves are so high. The water is rising. Soon we'll be eye to eye. Why am I so afraid to die when it takes more courage to live?

If I choose death, I'm giving up. I'm leaving and taking my baby with me. I'll also take a part of all the people who love me. Their lives will never be the same again.

Could I be a good mother? Will my daughter love me? Will she end up on a rock like this someday? I can only give her life; I can't give her paradise. I can't even give this child her daddy.

Gabriel, I don't want to leave you behind. Time will carry me far away. But I don't want to die. I want to break the chain of sadness. I'll miss you so much. It will be so painful. Maybe being alive is like having a baby; it hurts a lot, but it's worth it.

I've waited too long. The sea surrounds me. The steps leading back to the beach are gone. Jack is whimpering. I say, "Don't be afraid," and wrap my fingers around his collar. We can make it back to shore. If I have to die, Lord, I want to die trying to live.

Movement draws my eye to the side of the cliff. I know

those shoulders, that rangy build. Nobody else could've found this place. It was all a mistake. Gabe is here!

My vision clears. The man's face ages. Gabriel's father is plunging down the path, waving his arms and shouting. The path's too steep, he doesn't know the way, he's going to fall.

The waves are roaring. I'm raging at him: "Why did you come here? It's too late! You killed your son! I hate you!"

Then Jack and I leap into the water.

42

Francis McCloud

Jennie and the dog were facing the horizon. They didn't hear me shouting.

The path was slick. I kept slipping and sliding. The drop to the rocks below made me feel sick, but I had to keep going, I had to save her, even though I didn't know how. The tide would be too strong to fight. The steps were underwater. It's been too long; I don't remember where they are.

I am waving my arms. I am screaming her name. The waves break like thunder on Jennie's rock. Any second they'll pull her under.

Jennie turns around. She sees me. The look on her face almost makes me fall. I can see it plain, across the water. Her eyes are like Katherine's. They're awful.

She's shouting something I can't make out. Then she grabs the dog and jumps into the water.

The sight shoots inside my eyes and brands my brain. This is the hell that God has made me: Everything I touch dies, but I stay alive.

I search the waves, but Jennie is gone.

Too late. I've been too late all my life. My heart is bursting, I'm letting go, the sea reaches for me, I'm falling.

Jennie grabs my arm and pulls me back. I can't stand up, my legs don't work. Her eyes are as blue as the ocean. The dog runs up beside her and shakes himself. Water shoots off him like sparks of fire. Jennie's eyebrow is cut, she's crying blood. Beneath her wet dress, Jennie's belly is round.

I can't look in her eyes. I'm too ashamed. I know what she's thinking. She hates me.

Her hand comes down and gently touches my head.

"Don't worry, Mr. McCloud," she says. "I'll help you."

43

Jennie Harding

He drove me back to town. We didn't talk much. At one point he had to stop the truck. He was sobbing.

"I'm sorry," he said. "I was just so glad to see you."

"It's okay," I said, patting his arm. There was no room for hate inside me anymore. I was too full of Gabe. I was too full of sadness.

We had to stop for gas when we got to town.

"You'd think at a time like this . . . ," he said, embarrassed.

"There's no rush," I said. Jack was in the back, like a sack of wet laundry, his ears folded down, looking mournful.

My parents will expect me to be ashamed about the baby. They'll want me to put it up for adoption.

This is my baby and I'm going to keep it. I'll try to be a good mother. I know I'll make mistakes, but I'll always love her, and I'll tell her I love her every day of her life. Maybe the baby is the son that Gabriel wanted. A son would be fine. I'll tell my little boy: Being a man doesn't mean being big and tough. It means being big enough to be kind.

The past isn't going to go away. I'll always be connected to the McClouds. This child I'm carrying will be a member of their family. They'll love Gabe's baby as much as they know how; probably more than they could ever love each other.

It won't be perfect. I can't fix everything. I'm not a magician.

"We should get you to the doctor," Mr. McCloud said. "You're pretty banged up and that cut's still bleeding."

"I want to go home first." I knew I was okay. It would take more than death to kill me.

As we got near my house, Mr. McCloud slowed down. He said, "We want to help out with the baby. My wife and I—she always wanted to be a grandma. It's all we got left of Gabe."

"That's fine," I said.

He parked in front of my house. "I'll go in there with you, if you want me to."

"Thanks, but I can handle it," I told him.

He said, "I guess I better get home." I got out of the truck and he drove away.

I went up the front walk to the house I'd left that morning. That seemed like a million years ago. My childhood was over. And so was Gabe's. But I would survive and I would teach our child well. Our daughter or son will sing and laugh and play, and run along the beach, racing the waves. So will I, someday.

I opened the door.